ETERNAL BONDS

SUSAN HAYES

ABOUT THE BOOK

Duncan Masterson has a secret. To keep it, he's got a few simple rules. Stay away from sunlight, never drink from the unwilling, and never, ever get involved with mortals. It was working, until the night he finds a lovely co-worker dazed and bleeding from a vampire attack.

After decades as Duncan's guardian, Jared Evans has shared almost everything with Duncan, even regular doses of Duncan's blood to extend Jared's life. The only thing they've never shared was a woman...until Tabitha.

Rocked by revelations and faced with temptations she never imagined, Tabitha Blacke is flung headlong into a world full of danger, monsters, and two men who want to claim to her for eternity.

Etched In Stone

Eternal Bonds

Published by: Black Scroll Publications

ISBN: 978-1-988446-41-7

As always, this book is dedicated to my parents for believing in me, and to Karen, for her unwavering friendship, support, and a decade's worth of laughter. I couldn't do this without you guys.

CHAPTER 1

TABI KNEW BETTER than to be out in the parking lot this late into the night shift without an escort, but the only security guard available had been Darryl, and she'd be in more danger of getting attacked by his wandering hands than anyone lurking around the lot at four in the morning.

She got three steps out the door before she realized she'd forgotten to change her shoes, but by then she was ankle deep in snow. "Good job," she muttered to herself as the gray slush filled her flats and leeched the last warmth from her toes. As tempted as Tabi was to head back in and warm up, she'd never make it through her shift without something to eat, and she'd left her lunch in the car.

She trudged through the empty lot, watching the occasional snowflake swirl through the frozen night air. She had just started wondering how cold it needed to be for peanut butter to freeze when the hairs on the back of her neck stood up and she knew that she wasn't alone any longer. She kept walking, fighting to keep her pace regular, but she couldn't help hunching down into her jacket, as if the heavy wool could somehow protect her from whatever it was that had her instincts screaming at her to run. She fished her keys out of her pocket and tried to pick out the right one by feel alone as she made a discreet scan of the area near her car. She couldn't see anything, but she *knew* that there was someone nearby, watching her.

She was only a few feet from her car when she caught the faint sound of snow crunching underfoot somewhere behind her. With her heart pounding, she threaded the keys between the fingers of her hand just as she'd been taught in some long ago self-defense course and turned, prepared to fight for her life, only to find the parking lot as empty as ever, with only snow-covered cars for as far as the eye could see. She looked around, bewildered, but there was no one in sight and not so much as a shadow out of place.

"You've lost your ever-loving mind," she muttered to herself and turned back toward the car. That was when she finally saw him, and by then it was too late. Her screams never made it past the icy hand that clamped down over her mouth and her keys fell from nerveless fingers as she stared into a pair of soulless black eyes. Like a shark's. Part of her observed idly as her entire body stilled and a sense of inevitability flowed into her mind. This wasn't anything to be afraid of. It was all going to be all right, all she had to do was just let it happen—No! Tabi jerked her head away as she fought back, trying desperately to break free of the effect of those mesmerizing eyes.

She blinked and for a split second she could have sworn she saw a flicker of surprise, but then those twin pools of black burned into her mind and she felt herself falling into fathomless darkness. Inside her mind she clawed and screamed and fought, but Tabi could feel that it was futile, that her body had already surrendered and that somehow the fight was over before she had even begun.

It was the cold that she felt first, cold so bitter that it bordered on pain. Tabi moved her head just a little and tiny shards of crystalline fire burned and sizzled behind her eyes. "Ow," she moaned and was almost surprised when she heard her own voice.

That's a good sign, maybe I'm not dead after all.

Not feeling brave enough to risk opening her eyes just yet, Tabi did a slow, careful assessment of all her body parts and decided she seemed to be more or less in working order, though her neck was hurting like a son of a bitch. She was very cold, and her clothes were most definitely wet, but she was alive and that was not a bad start, all things considered. What the hell had happened to her attacker? One minute he was in her face and the next minute she was—Tabi realized she had no idea where she was. It was definitely time to open her eyes.

She cracked her eyes open and peeked around her, not sure what to expect. The area seemed empty. She lifted her head slightly and groaned as more stars bounced around her vision and filled her head with a hundred tiny sparks of pain. When the lights finally faded from her sight she sat up very slowly and quickly recognized where she was, flat on her ass, right beside her car. Why did her neck hurt so much? She reached up to check and pain shot through her the moment she touched her throat.

What the hell?

Tabi touched the area more gingerly this time, and her fingers came away glistening with blood. Her stomach churned and she took several quick, cleansing breaths. She knew it was crazy for her, a hospital admin assistant, to be queasy when it came to blood, but she was. Especially when that blood was her own.

Footsteps crunched through the slush and snow and Tabi hunkered down, inwardly mocking herself as she tried to scrunch her gangly five-foot-eleven-inch frame into a tiny ball. Every movement made her head hurt and waves of dizziness made it hard for her to think clearly, and Tabi knew she was losing body heat at an alarming rate. Please, be one of the good guys, she prayed silently. Right now she'd even welcome Darryl's groping fingers if it meant being helped back into the hospital where it was warm and safe.

"Ms. Blacke? Tabitha?" A man's voice called out her name and she felt a tingle that had nothing to do with the freezing temperature chase down her spine. "Tabitha, where are you?" There was only one man in the world who said her name with that delicious hint of Scottish brogue and Tabi breathed a sigh of relief. Dr. Duncan Masterson was a threat to her heart and her sanity, but he would never hurt her.

And here I am, bleeding in the snow with my shoes full of slush. Very sexy, Tabi.

"I'm over here, Dr. Masterson." Tabi's voice sounded unsteady even to her own ears, and she knew he'd have noticed. That man noticed everything. Well, almost everything. He seemed more or less oblivious to Tabi's existence apart from the occasional polite conversation when he needed to schedule a procedure or track down missing paperwork. A shame, because the good doctor starred in every one of Tabi's fantasies, and had since the day he'd started working at the hospital. *You're bleeding, cold, and wet, now is really not the time to lament your pathetic lack of a love life,* she reminded herself as Dr Masterson stepped into the space between the cars.

"Are you all right?" He crouched down beside her, strong hands already reaching out to examine her bloody throat. Even in the sickly orange glow of the sodium lighting there was no denying Duncan Masterson was a handsome man. He had a leonine quality to his face that was enhanced by the straight blond hair that he always wore tied back and tucked under the collar of his white coat. Tabi had often imagined what that mane of blond would look like if he wore it loose, just as she had fantasized about what it would feel like to run her hands through it while they—whoa. She put a halt on one of her favorite daydreams and dragged herself back to the present.

"Tabitha? I asked if you were all right. Did you hit your head?"

Tabi managed to unglue her tongue from the roof of

her mouth and form a few semi-coherent words. "I—I fell."

"Really?" He lifted his gaze from her throat and Tabi's breath caught as she found herself hopelessly lost in a pair of amber eyes. They were such an unusual shade, like dark honey or aged cognac, and there was something about the lighting that made them seem to glow.

"Tell me what really happened, lass." His brogue seemed thicker now, and Tabi felt each word glide over her like a physical caress.

"Someone attacked me. I tried to scream but his hand was over my mouth and he did this strange thing with his eyes and it made me want to stop fighting him. I tried to fight him off, but I couldn't." Tabi was speaking, but she couldn't remember actually making the decision to tell him anything. She certainly hadn't planned on it. Apart from her neck she was fine, if cold and wet, and her car keys were right there on the ground so she hadn't even been robbed. Her preliminary plan had been to claim she had been clumsy and fell, rather than have to deal with a police report and questions she'd rather not answer.

"And he did this to you?" Dr. Masterson lightly touched her neck but his eyes stayed firmly locked on hers.

"I don't know. I suppose so. I'm not even sure it was a man to be honest, Dr. Masterson. I didn't see anything but a pair of black, horrible eyes."

"Tell me about the eyes, Tabitha. Tell me everything you remember."

Tabi opened her mouth to speak, but then closed it

with a snap as a suspicion bloomed in her mind. "You're doing it, too!"

"Doing what?" Dr. Masterson's voice was saying one thing, but his eyes widened in surprise as she resisted whatever it was he was doing to her.

"That! It's what the other one did! Only your eyes are golden and his were black like a shark's. But you're both doing the same thing and I want you to stop it!" Tabi scrabbled backward, her hands plunging into the icy slush as she tried to put some distance between them. Until this second she'd always believed Dr. Duncan Masterson was a good man, but now she wasn't so sure.

"Incredible," he muttered and shook his head. "You shouldn't have been able to tell I was doing anything."

"I am not sure what the hell is going on here, but I'm cold, wet, and bleeding, and if you're done doing whatever you were doing, I'd like very much to get back inside and pretend this whole thing never happened."

"You would, would you?" Dr. Masterson grinned and Tabi's breath caught as his slow smile revealed that he'd been hiding a pair of sinfully sexy dimples behind his normally serious expression. Her stomach dipped and swirled and her thighs clenched together in response to that revelation and she mentally revised her assessment of him from handsome to panty-meltingly hot.

This is so not the time for this. Get up and get back inside before anything else weird happens!

"Yes. I'll just tell them I slipped and fell and that'll be the end of it." She was pleased to hear the steel was back in her voice. She started to get to her feet, but another wave of dizziness hit her and she sat back down again with a low moan of distress. "And that's what I'm going to do, just as soon as the Tilt-a-Whirl ride stops."

"I don't think so," he rumbled and before Tabi could muster up more than a surprised squawk Dr. Masterson had her in his arms and was lifting her up out of the snow.

"You can't carry me, I'm too heavy!"

"Never tell a man he can't do something, Tabitha. It's the surest way to make him try it, just to prove you wrong."

"Doctor, please, put me down. I'm not even sure I trust you after you did whatever that was back there a minute ago, and I certainly don't want to be seen being carried into the hospital looking like this."

"Well then, you're going to get your wish, or at least one of them." Duncan kept walking as he talked, cradling her to his chest.

"What?" Tabi felt a stab of panic and looked around her. "This isn't the way back to the hospital!"

"You said you didn't want to be seen being carried into the hospital like this, so we're not going back there."

"I said I didn't want to be carried into the hospital because I intended to walk, and I also said I didn't trust you and I can assure you that this is certainly not helping your case any! Now put me the fuck down!" Tabi snarled at him and started to thrash, but Duncan's arms could have been carved from marble for the amount of impact her struggling had on him.

"Did you just curse at me?" He paused to look down at her, his sensuous mouth quirked up into a grin that set his dimples on display again. "I didn't know that word was even part of your vocabulary."

"You've only met my work personality, doctor. I am very fucking capable of swearing, in multiple languages if I feel like it. Now put me down!"

There was no mistaking the flare of heat that shimmered in Duncan's eyes as he watched her struggle in the confines of his arms. "I'm sorry, but I can't. I know you don't trust me, but you should." He lifted her higher in his arms so that they were eye to eye. "I'll never hurt you, Tabitha. You have my oath on it."

She had meant to say something cutting, or at the very least argumentative, but as Tabi stared into his golden eyes she couldn't find the will to say anything at all. Instead she was drawn into the warmth and fire of his gaze, and the world faded away to nothing as she felt herself being wrapped in light and the promise of safety. Cocooned inside that golden shell, she finally stopped fighting and surrendered.

DUNCAN FELT the woman in his arms go limp as he broke down the last walls of her resistance. Humans who could resist the charms of a vampire existed of course, but it had been more than three quarters of a century since he'd actually met one. To discover that the shy and lovely Tabitha Blacke had that particular talent was a surprise, and one that made things a great deal more difficult for him at the moment since it meant there was no way he could wipe her memory of the night's events.

He settled Tabi's bruised and shivering body closer to his chest and started heading for his car, aware that he needed to get her out of sight before they were spotted. He had to take a good look at the bite on her throat and assess what the intent of her attacker had been.

Whoever they were, they'd been hunting on his turf. That would usually indicate a vampire fledgling, arrogant and driven by appetites that bordered on the obscene. Fledglings rarely left a living victim though, which made Duncan wonder if this was the opening move in a larger game. Tabitha sighed and stirred, burrowing her face against the warmth of his body and Duncan felt his cock harden in response. He'd wanted to have her in his arms like this for a long time, and now that he finally had her, Duncan was not sure he'd ever be willing to let her go.

She had held his attention from the first time he'd seen her, quiet and solitary as she had made her way through the cafeteria lunch line up, her head down and her shoulders hunched in a vain attempt to disguise her height. He knew her habits, at least at work. He had learned when she took her breaks, and where her favorite places were to hide when the chaos got to be too much. He even knew the sight of blood made her queasy, despite how hard she worked to conceal the fact from her co-workers. He'd spent months getting to know her, and yet until tonight they'd barely exchanged more than a few dozen words. He had fought his own desires and stayed away from her because he didn't want her to be tainted by the darkness of his world.

As he gently lowered her into the backseat of his car he wondered if the universe was laughing at him now, because here they were after all. For better or worse, she was irrevocably part of his world now because her mind was too strong for the usual compulsions to take hold. He could make her sleep for a time, but he couldn't wipe her memories of what had transpired tonight. And if he was going to be honest with himself, he was happy that was the case. After months and months of watching her from a distance, of only getting to have her in his dreams, he was finally going to have a chance to spend time with Tabitha. He just hoped she didn't hate him for it.

Once she was curled up on the seat, Duncan dialed the hospital and let them know that Ms. Blacke from administration had fallen in the parking lot and that he'd volunteered to drive her home. It was near the end of his shift and the place was quiet, so there was no issue with him leaving early. With that detail handled, he dialed another number and settled into the driver's seat of his Mercedes as he waited for Jared to answer the phone. He was going to need some help dealing with Tabitha once she woke up.

Jared answered the phone with a sleepy drawl. "You had better be lying in a ditch somewhere right now, more than a little bit dead. Do you have any idea what time it is?"

Seventy-six years they'd been together and Jared still complained every single morning. "It's only an hour before my shift ends, and is that any way to talk to your employer? Get up, Jared, I need you," Duncan barked into the phone, keeping his voice low enough there was no chance it would disturb Tabi.

Instantly the voice on the other end of the line was all business. "What do you need? Are you okay?"

"I'm fine, but one of the hospital employees was just attacked by another vampire."

Jared sighed and then asked, "Do you need me to help you deal with the body?"

"No. Whoever her attacker was they left her alive, but weak. I need to take a better look and I can't do that here. I'm bringing her home."

"Here?" Jared choked. "You never bring anyone here. Ever. What aren't you telling me? And who the hell would be so ballsy as to hunt in your own backyard?"

"I'm not sure what's going on yet, or who's involved, but I'm not happy, that's for damned sure. As for why I'm bringing her home..." Duncan sighed and scrubbed a hand over his stubbled jaw. "They went after Tabitha, and apparently the two of you have something in common."

Jared was silent for a moment and then swore out loud as he worked out what the problem was. "Tabitha, the one you've been mooning after like a poleaxed steer for the past year, that Tabitha? And you can't wipe her memory?"

Duncan sighed as he recalled the strength of her will as he tried to get her to go to sleep. "I could barely put her under at all, and apparently neither could whoever attacked her."

"I'll get one of the spare bedrooms ready. Congratulations, after all these years we're finally going to have a house guest, maybe now you'll stop being such a grouch."

"I am not a grouch, thank you. I'm a bloody saint, putting up with the mouthiest man—"

"You call me your manservant and you'll be heating your own meals for a month. And you've been damned grumpy ever since you laid eyes on Tabitha and decided you weren't going to sully up her pretty little world with your issues, so quit denying it. Just bring her here and we'll figure it out, boss."

"Make sure you double check the wards on the windows and doors too, will you? I'm pretty certain they're going to be tested soon."

"You got it. See you in thirty minutes." Jared paused and then added, "Have you eaten tonight?"

"A few hours ago. I'm fine."

"Right. And the smell of her blood in your car isn't affecting you at all. I'll make sure there's a hot meal waiting for you here."

"Thanks."

"Just don't eat her on the way home. I'm looking forward to having someone around here who actually appreciates my cooking."

"She's not staying with us long, so don't you go getting attached." Even as he said it, Duncan knew he was fooling himself. If he had his way, Tabi would be staying forever.

"That's what you said about me, boss, and I've been here seventy-five years now."

"Seventy-six to be exact. And that's precisely my point. I do not need another pain in the ass human cluttering up the place. One of you is more than enough, thank you."

"Whatever you say, boss. See you soon."

"I'll be there before your espresso is finished."

Duncan ended the call and turned in his seat so he could look at Tabi. She was still asleep, her face pale and her clothing soaked with water and blood. Her long legs were drawn up into a loose fetal position and tendrils of her auburn hair were plastered to her cheek and neck. She looked beautiful and terribly vulnerable, too. Duncan started the engine, turned the heater up, and then flipped on the rear seat-warmers. He couldn't do anything about dry clothes, but at least he could make sure she was warm.

For one fleeting instant he considered crawling into the backseat to hold her in his arms for just a little while, but he dismissed the thought at once. Jared was right. The scent of her blood was intoxicating and it was stirring both his need and his hunger, tempting him to do the unthinkable.

Duncan's fingers tightened on the steering wheel. He had his code, and he lived by it, and rule number one was that he never drank from the unwilling. Even though they never remembered a thing afterward, he always got their permission first. He smiled to himself. Permission was probably not the right word. Usually they begged him to do anything, to take anything he wanted, so long as the pleasure didn't end.

CHAPTER 2

TABI HAD NEARLY WOKEN up on the way home and Duncan had been forced to pull over and send her back to sleep. It had been confirmation of what he had already known. There was going to be no way to wipe her memory of the night's events.

He pulled up to the house and noted that Jared had turned on the outside flood lights, making the driveway and the path up to the house almost daylight bright. By the time Duncan had Tabi in his arms Jared was at the door, his expression grim as he scanned the area, a shotgun held loosely at his side.

"A shotgun? Really?" Duncan shook his head as he made his way up the stairs with his precious burden held close to his body to shield her from the light snow that had started just before they'd arrived.

"My own special recipe. The shells are loaded with silver nitrate and garlic." Jared gave him a grin and moved aside, closing the door behind them.

"You have that in *my* house? When were you going to tell me?" Duncan was old enough that not even sunlight was a true threat to him anymore, never mind garlic, but the habits of several hundred years of living were not easy to break.

"There didn't seem to be any point in telling you until I actually had a reason to use it. Now I've got a reason." Jared shrugged his massive shoulders. "I've been preparing for something like this for a long time. You don't keep me around just to heat your meals up for you, we both know that. I'm your guardian. What kind of guardian would I be if I didn't have a contingency plan?"

"When this is over you and I are going to have a chat about these contingency plans of yours. I like knowing what's going on in my household."

Jared laughed and fell in behind Duncan. "And I like waking up to the smell of grits and frying bacon, but the only way that's going to happen around here is if I make it myself. We don't always get what we want, boss."

Duncan looked down at Tabi, her dark lashes fanning her cheeks as she slept with her head resting on his shoulder. "Sometimes, though, it might be that we do."

TABI WOKE UP AND STRETCHED, feeling blissfully warm. It was only when she opened her eyes that the bliss melted away and left her gawking around a room that was most definitely *not* her cramped bedroom in her equally cramped apartment. She sat up and a familiar sense of dizziness hit her, and along with it came a recollection of what had happened before she'd inexplicably conked out.

"Tabitha? Tabi, you need to move slowly." A familiar voice drew her attention and she turned her head to find Duncan Masterson, ER doctor and apparently part-time kidnapper, standing a few feet away, watching her with concern.

"You!" Tabi ignored Duncan's instructions and moved as fast as she could, so quickly in fact that she was halfway out of bed before she noticed she wasn't wearing any clothes. With a cry of shock she dove back under the covers again and hid, her neck burning and her head spinning from her sudden exertions. "You just stay away from me! Stay away, give me back my clothes and let me out of here! Right *now*!"

"Tabi, calm down. You were attacked. I brought you to my house to take care of you." Duncan raised his hands, trying to placate her.

"Calm down? No, I will not calm down. I'm *naked*! Some freak attacked me in the parking lot, cut my neck, and now I'm naked at your house. What part of that is supposed to inspire a sense of tranquility?"

"I see our guest is awake," a new voice drawled and Tabi turned toward the sound. Standing in the doorway was the biggest stereotype of a Texas rancher she had ever seen. He was huge, standing well over six feet tall, with short, red-blond hair that would have been curly if it were just a little longer. His face was dusted with freckles, his gray-green eyes were full of laughter, and all that was missing was for him to be chewing on a stalk of hay.

"Who the hell are you?" she demanded as she reined

in her hormones, which were busy making all sorts of calculations about what he looked like under the form-fitting sweater and blue jeans he was wearing. "And where are my clothes!"

"I thought you said she was a quiet, mousy little thing, boss. You sure this is her?"

"Shut up, Jared. You're not helping matters."

"Mousy?" Tabi looked back at Duncan, still smarting from the insult. "You tell people I'm mousy?! I'm not mousy, I'm professional! And why are you talking about me at all, Dr. Masterson? Didn't your mother teach you that if you can't say anything nice about someone you shouldn't say anything at all? And here I thought you were always such a gentleman!"

The man Duncan had called Jared started to laugh, the rich, warm tones filling the room and drowning out her angry accusations. When he finally stopped laughing he took a step into the room and touched his hand to an invisible hat brim in greeting. "I like you already, Tabitha. My name is Jared Evans. I work for Dr. Masterson. Your clothes were soaking wet and covered in blood, so I took the liberty of putting them in the wash for you while the doc cleaned up that, uh, cut on your neck."

"So you both stripped me naked and then stole my clothes, lovely!" Her heart was hammering against her ribs and she wasn't sure whether it was because of the strange turn her night had taken or the fact that two mouthwateringly hot men had taken off her clothes and tucked her into bed. She decided it was probably both.

"Tabitha, you need to calm down. You've lost a lot of blood and you're going to put too much stress on your body. That's why you keep getting dizzy, lass." Duncan's accent deepened again and he took several steps toward the bed. "I swear to you, you're safe. You were so cold and wet I had to take off your clothes, yes, but you were covered with a blanket the whole time. It had to be done, and you were still unconscious."

A fragment of a memory niggled at the back of her mind and Tabi's eyes widened as she remembered the rest of what had happened. "You did that to me! You made me go to sleep. I remember now. You stared at me and it was like I was hypnotized."

"Yes." Duncan didn't even bother to deny it. "I did that to you, because you were frightened and hurt and I needed to get you to safety. There wasn't time for proper explanations."

Tabi opened her mouth, then closed it again, not certain what to say to that. It was a lot easier to keep yelling than it was to actually try and deal with everything that had happened. But she'd known Duncan Masterson for more than a year, and until tonight he'd seemed perfectly normal. So maybe she should give him a chance to explain. "So I'm just supposed to trust you? Is that it?"

"Yes." Duncan gave her another one-word answer and Tabi felt her irritation start to rise again.

"Trust is earned. You can start by getting me something to wear, and then you can explain to me why you brought me here instead of just treating me at the hospital. *Then* you can explain what the hell happened tonight, because I'm starting to think you know a lot more than you're telling me."

Duncan glanced over at Jared, who grinned and nodded. "Clothes for the lady, I'm on it." As he walked out of the room Tabi heard the telltale sound of boot heels hitting hardwood and she grinned. The cowboy was even wearing cowboy boots. *And he's got a nice ass, too,* the hormone-driven portion of her brain noted before she could shut it off again.

She turned her attention back to Duncan and realized he'd moved to her side in the brief second she'd been distracted. She hadn't heard or seen him move though, and having him so close was decidedly unsettling. Maybe overwhelming desire was a rare side-effect of being attacked or maybe it was just the fact she'd been lusting after him for a year, but either way she was having a hard time thinking clearly when he was close enough to touch.

"Dr. Masterson, you really need to take a few steps back. Better yet, you could leave the room completely."

He stayed just where he was, just enough of a smile on his handsome face that one of his dimples was showing. "Call me Duncan."

"What I should be doing is calling the police right now." Tabi reached behind her to grab another pillow to pile between her and the headboard, but Duncan took it from her and held it, clearly waiting for her to lean forward so he could place it for her.

"Duncan, you need to put that down and leave me alone, please?"

He shook his head and lifted a hand to her bare shoulder, running the back of his fingers across her skin in a coaxing caress. "Let me help you, Tabi. I know you don't trust me, but I believe you will, in time. At least I hope so."

His touch sent flickers of flame dancing over Tabi's flesh, and she had to bite her lip to stop herself from doing something foolish. Instead she merely leaned forward, allowing him to settle the pillow behind her, feeling very vulnerable as she exposed her naked back to him. The hand on her shoulder moved downward, brushing her hair out of the way as he ran his knuckles lightly over her shoulder blade.

"You have scars?"

Damn. I'd forgotten about them.

Tabi leaned back into the pillows, trapping Duncan's hand behind her but effectively blocking his view. His hand was warm where it rested against her skin, and she belatedly realized that in their new position, he'd been pulled even closer to her. *Not good.* She lifted her gaze and found herself staring into his amber eyes again, but this time there was no strange glow, only the heat of what she swore was desire.

Desire for me?

"Circular burn scars. From a cigarette?" he asked, making no attempt to remove his hand.

"I don't want to talk about it."

Duncan just nodded and she was relieved to note his eyes still gleamed with interest and not with pity. "I am not bothered by them."

Tabi just shrugged. "You may not be bothered by them, but I am. They're a reminder of a time in my life I don't like to think about."

"Then don't think." He leaned in closer, his mouth

capturing hers in a torrid kiss. This was not a gentle caress but a full-on sensual assault, his lips slanted across hers, possessing and claiming her as his fingers speared into her hair, wrapping it around his fist as he moved in closer, pushing her back into the pillows.

Tabi's thoughts scattered like dandelion fluff in a hurricane as his need swept through her and kindled her own desires. His kiss was better than any erotic daydream she had ever cast him in. The reality of his touch was so much more than she could have ever imagined. She wrapped an arm around his shoulders, feeling the powerful muscles beneath her hand, wanting to experience everything that he was. He growled, low and deep in his chest and it stirred up the memory of what had happened to her only a short time before. His growl echoed the one that she'd heard just as she'd been attacked, and the recollection was enough to bring Tabi back to her senses.

She'd wanted this for so long. Wanted Duncan to notice her.

But not like this.

She could hardly believe her own actions as she turned her head, breaking their kiss as she unwound her arm from his shoulders and released him. "No." Surprise and confusion clouded his beautiful eyes and made the passion that had been burning there dwindle down to embers, but she held to her resolve. There were too many questions still unanswered, and she was pretty damned sure that she wasn't going to like at least some of the answers.

"Tabi."

"I said no." She moved even further back, putting space between them.

"I'm not used to being told no."

"You're a doctor and a very handsome man, I'm sure you don't hear it often. But that doesn't change the fact I said it."

"After you kissed me," Duncan pointed out.

"I'm having a bad day, but I'm not dead. A woman would have to be a week past her expiry date not to react when a hot man kisses her like that."

Duncan ran a hand through his hair, loosening it enough that strands fell around his face as he gave her a look of pure frustration, "You just called me handsome and hot in the last thirty seconds, lass. Are ye sure the answer's still no?"

Tabi's pussy quivered at his accented words and she had to tangle her fingers in the sheets to stop from reaching out to brush his hair back from his face. She knew if she touched him again she'd never find the strength to stop a second time.

She was saved from answering Duncan's question by Jared's return. He announced his arrival with a knock on the doorframe, and when she glanced up she saw he had an armload of clothes and a knowing smirk on his face. Clearly he'd overheard at least part of their conversation.

"I found our guest some clothes. It's nothing fancy, ma'am, but I've got a few things for you to try on, I'm sure something will fit. Then I fixed you some breakfast, hot biscuits, and coffee."

"That sounds fantastic, thank you. And thanks for the clothes. I really will feel better once I'm dressed again. "

"My pleasure." Jared touched that invisible hat brim again and then placed the jumble of clothes at the foot of the bed. "You just come on downstairs when you're ready. We'll be in the kitchen."

"I had intended to stay and help Tabi dress. She's still weak," Duncan avoided looking her in the eye as he said it, and Tabi found herself getting irritated all over again. She sat up quickly, intent on proving she was fine, but the rapid motion made her head whirl and she groaned as the bedroom started spinning again.

"You see? You need to stay in bed and rest. We can talk later, after you've slept." Duncan reached for her and she slapped his hand away.

"I'm not going back to sleep again. And don't you *dare* try to make me. I'm getting up, getting dressed, and coming downstairs to have something to eat and some coffee. God in heaven do I need coffee." Tabi glanced at Duncan's glowering face and made a snap decision. She had to get some space from him before she did something she'd regret, like kissing him again. Not that she was really regretting that first kiss, but she wasn't exactly in her right mind right now either. "Since you seem to be right about my being weak still, I have a solution. Jared can stay and help me."

"No," Duncan ground out the single word from between clenched teeth.

"Either he stays, or you both leave and I'll manage on my own."

"Fine, have it your way." Duncan got up off the bed and headed for the door, nearly bumping shoulders with Jared as he passed him. "Upset her and we won't make seventy-seven," he muttered and then he was gone, pulling the door closed behind him with enough force to shudder the doorframe.

"You'll have to forgive him, he's not really himself at the moment, ma'am," Jared explained, jerking his head over his shoulder toward the door.

"Call me Tabi. And I'm not myself at the moment either," she told him as she stayed still, waiting for the dizziness to fade.

"Then you can call me Jared. We're not very formal 'round here. No need, since I'm the only other person living here." Jared started looking through the clothes he'd brought while she took her first good look around the room she'd woken up in. The walls were painted a buttery cream and accented with a deep burgundy trim, and the blood-red quilt she was currently hiding under was edged in gold to match the room. A heavy wooden dresser stood against one wall, and a single, upholstered chair sat in one corner with a footstool at its base. The walls were bare though, and there was a lack of warmth to the room that told her it was normally empty.

Jared finished picking out clothes and held up a dark-green sweater. When she nodded in approval he brought it over to her side of the bed and handed it to her. "Try that. It'll likely be big enough for two of you, but it'll keep you warm and let you stay covered up while we find something for the bottom half."

She took the offered sweater and pulled it over her head, immediately sensing the sandalwood and citrus scent that Duncan wore. This was his then. She couldn't pretend that the idea of wearing Duncan's clothing didn't appeal to her, and Tabi snuggled into the cocoon of soft wool with a happy sigh.

Jared watched her and then smiled a little. "Duncan's a good man, and he's been talking about you for a long time now. Having you here has just thrown him off his stride. When he called and told me you'd been hurt, well, I'd never heard him so worried before."

"He talked about me? Are you sure? He's barely spoken to me before tonight. You must be mistaken."

"No mistake. And it's not my place to tell you the reasons for what he did," Jared winked at her. "And what he hasn't done up until now. He'll explain it all to you soon."

"I hope so. I...I like him. I always have. I just never knew him very well." Tabi sat up slowly and Jared reached out, offering her his hand. She took it with a grateful smile, aware of how his hand dwarfed hers when they were put together. He helped her up, and when she wobbled slightly he drew her against the broad wall of his chest and held her there until she felt steady on her feet.

"You're taller than I expected," he murmured, his voice a soft buzz near her ear that made her pulse flutter. "And there's more fire in you than he let on."

"He didn't know me well enough to have ever seen that part of me, and I know I'm too tall. I can't help it."

"Too tall? No. You're perfect. I would barely have to lower my head to kiss those sweet lips of yours."

Tabi froze and her body stiffened as she realized what Jared had just said. "But I thought you said it was Duncan who liked me."

"He does. Does that mean I can't like you, too?" Jared nuzzled her hair and Tabi felt a wash of liquid heat spread out from her womb as she responded to the big man's touch.

"I'm pretty sure that's supposed to be how it works," she managed to stammer, not at all sure what was going on. "He's your boss!"

"He is, and he isn't. We have a complicated arrangement. He'll explain that to you too."

"Why is it that everything about you two is complicated?" Tabi demanded.

"I thought women liked complicated men." Jared swept her hair back from her ear and began nibbling her earlobe.

"I—we—you should stop that."

"Probably, but I'm not going to. Not until you tell me to, just like you told Duncan."

Tabi's cheeks flamed as she realized that Jared had heard and seen more than she had first suspected. "All right then, Jared, I want you to—"

He cut her off before she could utter another word. His kiss was different from Duncan's but just as demanding, accepting nothing less than her complete surrender. His lips were fuller and he tasted of peppermint, the tingling coolness filling her mouth as he swept his tongue along the seam of her lips. Large, strong hands splayed across her back, holding her close as another wave of dizziness washed over her and left her weakened in its wake.

When he lifted his head and drew a ragged breath, Tabi did the same. Once she had refilled her lungs she laid a hand on his chest and pushed. "I was going to tell you no."

"I know. That's why I stopped you from talking." He glanced down at her hand and grinned. "You're going to need to push a whole lot harder than that if you want me to get away from you, honey. "

"Please let me go? I need to finish getting dressed, and then apparently I'm going to go downstairs and someone is finally going to tell me what the hell is going on." She tipped her head up slightly to look Jared in the eye. "And just so you and I are very clear on something, I don't care what weird arrangement you and your *boss* have, I don't have any intention of being a part of it."

"Until you arrived, Duncan and I didn't have any kind of arrangement when it came to women. Hell, there hasn't been a woman here in a very long time."

"What do you mean there hasn't been a woman here? You're both gorgeous, and clearly you're not gay... So what's the problem?"

Jared loosened his hold on her, watching her carefully to make sure she kept her balance. "This is our home, and our sanctuary. You'll understand how important that is later on. For right now, let's just say that until you came along, this wasn't even a consideration. And it's possible that when Duncan finds out I kissed you, he's going to tear my head off, so this may all be a moot point." He smoothed his hands down her hips, tugging down the sweater to mid-thigh. "Sit down and I'll see if I have something in this mess to cover up those lovely legs of yours, though I'd be a very happy man if you decided to go downstairs just as you are."

"That is not going to happen, buster. Dream on. It's the middle of winter, and I'm trapped with two men who seem to want me, and those are some very good reasons for not wandering around without any pants."

"Oh sure, bring logic into it." Jared sighed and gave her legs a last, lingering look that made her pussy clench and her heart race. "Yep, that view's definitely worth dying for."

"Don't be ridiculous, Duncan isn't going to hurt you, he doesn't have any claim on me at all. He's known me for more than a year and never shown any interest before now. One kiss is hardly a declaration of possession."

Jared just grinned and fished out a pair of gray track pants. "You might find he has a differing opinion. These should do the trick." He knelt at her feet and produced a pair of thick woolen socks that he tugged up over her feet. Once her toes were covered he very gently slipped the pants on and drew them up to her knees before letting her take over. "I'll just give you a second to get them pulled up the rest of the way." He winked at her and stood up, deliberately turning his back so she had privacy to finish dressing. The pants were a little too long, but once she cinched the drawstring around her waist, they were comfortable enough.

"You can turn around now."

Jared glanced back over his shoulder and laughed. "Duncan on top and me on the bottom, how appropriate."

As Tabi blushed and tried to figure out what on earth she could say in response, Jared turned, scooped her into his arms as though she weighed nothing at all, and headed for the door. "Time for us to have some breakfast, those biscuits are going to be cold if we don't get down there soon."

Tabi didn't bother arguing with Jared's plan to carry her downstairs because she just didn't have the energy. Instead she closed her eyes and pressed her cheek against the soft fibers of Jared's sweater, letting the spicy musk of his scent distract her from the ongoing insanity that had made up the night so far.

CHAPTER 3

Jared took his time carrying Tabi downstairs to the kitchen. He enjoyed having her in his arms, probably more than he should, considering Duncan's interest. In all the years he'd been in Duncan's service, their tastes had never intersected when it came to a woman, probably because neither of them was looking for more than a short-term fling. In Duncan's case, very short-term.

Like the amount of time it took him to fuck, feed, and make the girl forget him.

Jared could already sense that the hazel-eyed beauty in his arms was going to change all that.

Tabi stirred and her pretty eyes opened again as he took the last stair and turned toward the kitchen. "You sighed. Is something wrong?"

"I did?" Jared hadn't even noticed. "No, nothing's wrong. I guess I was just mourning the fact I'm going to have to put you down in a second."

"Ha! More likely you were wondering if your back

31

was going to give out before we got to the table. I'm not exactly pocket-sized."

"Nope. I already told you, you're perfectly sized."

"The rest of the world doesn't agree with you."

"So? Honey, you have two men right here who are in complete agreement about this."

"Agreement about what?" Duncan asked and his eyes narrowed as he saw Jared carrying Tabi into their spacious kitchen. Jared noted the response and bit back a chuckle. Duncan's sexually charged vampire nature was finally reemerging. All it had taken was nearly eighty years of sulking and a long-legged beauty named Tabi.

"I was just telling Tabi that she's the perfect size, just tall enough to kiss without a man having to bend over double." Duncan's eyes blazed golden fire and Jared knew he'd struck home. "All right, honey. I'll set you down at the table and I'll grab us both some food and coffee." Jared glanced at Duncan. "Did you eat already?"

"Yes," Duncan snapped, still looking decidedly displeased at the attention Jared was paying to Tabi.

"Great, then you keep our guest company while I get the food organized." Jared settled Tabi into one of the kitchen chairs and gave her a wink that made her blush faintly. That trace of pink sent a jolt of lust slamming straight to his dick and Jared had to turn away quickly before Tabi got an eyeful of the rock-hard evidence of his interest.

He barely got two steps away before he caught a deep, primal growl that was pitched too low for Tabi's human ears to catch. Jared heard it just fine though, thanks to the enhanced abilities Duncan's blood gave him, and the message was very clear. Duncan's interest in Tabi was escalating rapidly, and he didn't seem to appreciate Jared's flirtations. What Duncan hadn't yet realized was that Jared wasn't just flirting. He was truly attracted to her, both for her looks and her spirit.

Jared set down the trays of biscuits, bacon, and eggs he'd made for them both and took a seat across from Tabi, noticing that Duncan had moved a chair around so he was at her side.

"Thanks. I'm starved. That was actually why I was out in the parking lot when I got attacked. I'd left my lunch in the car." Tabi attacked her meal with enthusiasm, and Jared grinned as he watched her eat. He hadn't cooked for anyone but himself for too long, and it was a pleasure to have someone to share a meal with. Duncan preferred to consume the heated blood packs he acquired from the hospital and other sources in private, and he always hunted alone.

When Jared had given Tabi time to refuel, he took the bull by the horns and initiated the conversation he sensed neither she nor Duncan was willing to start. "How's your neck feeling?"

She raised a hand to the gauze that covered the torn flesh of her throat. "It's okay. It twinges if I move my head too much, but it's not bad. I'm not sure what I'm going to tell them at the office though. If I say I was attacked, there's going to be a fuss." Tabi's eyes widened. "Work. Oh my god! I vanished in the middle of my shift! They're going to fire me!"

"No, they're not," Duncan interjected. "I let them

know you'd injured yourself and that I had volunteered to take you home."

"You didn't tell them I was attacked, did you?" Tabi paled and Jared noticed she was gripping her fork so tightly her knuckles had turned white.

"Would that have been a problem, honey?" Jared asked, sensing there was something else going on here.

"What?" Tabi's gaze jerked up from her food to Jared and he read a myriad of emotions playing over her sweet face. Guilt, unease and...fear? Jared set down his coffee and leaned back in his chair, fighting the urge to wrap her in his arms and offer to protect her from whatever it was that had made her so afraid.

"Why wouldn't you want anyone to know you were attacked? What were you going to tell them happened to you?"

"I—"

Duncan cut her off. "You said you were going to tell them you fell. I had forgotten about that. Why wouldn't you just tell the truth?"

"Because the truth involves a police report, and questions, and well...I'd rather just avoid all that."

"As would I," Duncan admitted and Jared caught the look of surprise on Tabi's face at that confession. "But before we get into my reasons, I'd like to hear yours."

Tabi looked panicked and Jared was on his feet before he could think twice. She was already rising out of her chair by the time he reached her and by then he and Duncan had her pressed between them, their hands on her shoulders to prevent her from bolting from the room.

She stared first at Duncan and then Jared, and belatedly Jared realized both of them had reacted too quickly for her to have even seen them move.

Shit.

ONE MINUTE they'd all been sitting around the table and the next minute Tabi found herself the filling in a man-sandwich straight out of her wildest fantasies. She dragged a hit of air into her lungs and caught the scent of both men as they surrounded her. Her breasts instantly tightened and her pussy tingled as she felt the hard, muscled bodies of both men press into her. Two hot, handsome bodies that had moved so fast they'd been a blur. That thought snapped her back to the present with a crash.

"Let me go!"

"No, lass. Not until you've calmed down."

"You're telling me to calm down again? Didn't you learn anything from the last time we had this conversation? You can't just tell me to be calm every time the weird-shit-meter hits eleven!"

She felt Jared's chest vibrate with laughter and she turned her head to glower at him. "And you! Care to explain how you did that? No one moves that fast unless they're from the planet Krypton!"

"Boss? I think we're going to have to explain."

"Indeed," Duncan sighed. "Did you have to move like that? You scared her."

"Me? You were the one who had her ready to bolt like a scalded cat!"

"Guys? Hello? *She* is standing right here and she'd really like some answers!" Tabi was getting tired of being talked about like she didn't have ears. In an attempt to get some breathing room she worked a hand between herself and each of their chests intent on pushing them away, but the act of rubbing her way up their hard bodies started another line of thinking altogether. Her thoughts derailed into a pileup of hot fantasies and lust, and instead of pushing she simply left her fingers splayed across two solid walls of male muscle.

Both men pushed in closer, until she was caught between twin pillars of sex and heat that had her blood simmering and her brain mushy. Jared covered her hand with his so that it was held firmly just over his heart while Duncan turned her until his mouth could capture hers. This time his kiss was gentle, tender and intended to comfort, and Tabi was too overwhelmed by her desires to do anything else but tangle her fingers into Duncan's shirt and pull him in closer as she answered his kiss in kind.

Jared lifted his hand from her shoulder to sweep her hair back from her neck, dropping delicate kisses along the edge of the bandage.

"Mine," Duncan growled in warning and tugged her harder against him, pulling her a half step away from Jared.

"No," Jared growled back and moved in behind her, sandwiching her between them.

Duncan lifted his head and Tabi gasped as she saw his eyes. They were incandescent, glowing so brightly that it was as if there was a fire burning inside him.

This time Tabi did push away from him, straight back into Jared's arms.

"What are you?" She managed to keep from screaming the question at Duncan, hanging onto her sanity by the barest of threads. What the hell had she just been kissing?

Jared wrapped his arms around her and stepped back from Duncan, taking Tabi with him. "Boss, you need to chill."

Who were these two, the masters of understatement? "No, he needs to stop growling and glowing and tell me what the hell is going on! And both of you need to stop kissing me until I get some answers. My brain doesn't work well when it's drowning in hormones." Oh god, she just said that out loud.

"Hormones?" Both men echoed her last word and Tabi nearly screamed with frustration. "Out of everything I said, you two focused on that word?" she snapped and tried pulling herself out of Jared's embrace. She managed to twist slightly, but that was all. He was impossibly strong.

"This is going well," Jared quipped in rueful tones.

"You're not helping," Duncan snarled, revealing a pair of long canines as he ran a hand through his hair, pulling it out of its customary tie. His eyes were only glowing a little now, but Tabi was too busy staring at his mouth and fighting Jared's hold to really notice.

"You've got fangs? When did you get fangs?"

"Oh yeah, this is going fucking brilliantly." Jared tightened his hold on Tabi and dropped his mouth to her ear. "It's all right, honey. Neither of us is going to hurt you, but you're going to hurt yourself if you keep struggling."

Tabi stopped trying to get away and went still, finally accepting there was no point, not when Jared was so much stronger than she was. "Answers. I want answers right now or I'm going to start screaming."

"Sure thing," Jared drawled and loosened his hold on her slightly as he nuzzled her hair. "Duncan there is a three hundred year old vampire and I've been his guardian and companion for more than seventy-five years. You got your throat torn open by another vampire, and that's why Duncan had to bring you back here."

She'd heard enough, these men were insane. Tabi drove her heel into Jared's instep and let herself sag straight down, slipping partially out of his arms before he could recover. She gathered her strength and used all the power in her long legs to drive herself up and away from Jared, breaking free and sprinting for the back door she had noticed earlier. Better sock feet in the snow and risk freezing to death than to spend another minute in this house.

She didn't even make it to the door. Something large and moving impossibly fast passed her and then turned to block her way and she screamed as she slammed into it. She lashed out with her fists, but it felt like she was punching stone. Her hands hurt but she didn't seem to be making any impression. She slashed out with her finger-nails, desperate to get away, but someone caught her wrists, drawing her arms behind her as she fought and screamed again. Tabi felt herself being lifted and she kicked with both feet, hearing a grunt of pain as she connected with flesh.

Good, I hope that hurt! she thought to herself as the blur in front of her took shape and she realized she was staring up into Duncan's golden eyes. He looked pissed. He also looked incredibly turned on, and the look he was giving her had Tabi's knees trembling with something other than fear. He didn't look like he wanted to hurt her. He looked like he wanted to fuck her senseless. Holy shit, she was in serious trouble.

"Enough!" Duncan commanded, and Tabi felt her body obeying instantly.

"Stop doing that!" she snarled, too angry to question the wisdom of challenging someone who had fangs and eyes that glowed. Instantly she felt control of her body return to her. That was when she noticed he had four fresh scratches running down his cheek.

"You clawed me." Duncan touched his face and brought away his fingers with a look of surprise as he spotted the traces of blood on the tips.

"You kidnapped me, stripped me naked, and then started growling and sporting fangs, and you're worried that I scratched you and messed up your handsome face? Really? In my book we are not even close to being even yet," Tabi grumbled, trying to ignore the fact that his hair was down and his mouth was inches from hers and if she just leaned forward a little—what the hell was wrong with her? He was a psycho! Hadn't she had enough of dangerous, controlling men in her life?

"Mousy my ass. You brought home a hell cat, boss. I think we should seriously consider—"

"Not another word, Jared. You've said quite enough. Tabi, I apologize. This was not how I wanted to do this."

Tabi managed to rein in her out of control libido and corral her scattered wits. "Do what? Make sure I need a lifetime's worth of counseling? Scare me half to death? Just let me go, please? I promise I won't tell anyone anything."

"Come to the living room and we'll talk. I've already given you my word no harm will come to you. I know you don't have any reason to, but I need you to trust me. To trust us."

"Remember what I said about trust being earned? You two currently have a negative balance." She tugged at her wrists, still pinned behind her back by Jared. "At least let go of me. You've made it abundantly clear there's no point in trying to run away. Whatever you are, you're both too strong and too fast to be human."

"I told you, he's a vampire and I'm his guardian. That was the truth," Jared told her as he released her wrists.

"You're clearly not the diplomat in this arrangement," Tabi grumped and stepped sideways so there was finally a bit of space between her and the two men who seemed determined to turn her on and then terrify her.

"I'm the brawn, not the brains," Jared told her, chuckling.

"That doesn't make any sense. If he's the vampire," she pointed to Duncan. "Shouldn't he be stronger than you?"

"When he's awake he is. But even vampires need their naps."

"I do not *nap!*" Duncan snapped. "Now, can we please

go to the living room and we'll try and do this like civilized folks and not babbling barbarians." He shot Jared a look of pure annoyance and Tabi caught herself on the verge of giggling.

I'm losing my mind. There is no way I should be finding any of this funny.

Both men reached for her and she darted out of their grasp, determined to keep her distance until she had some answers. "Point me to the living room and I'll make my own way, thank you." She'd make it there under her own steam, even if she had to crawl. Every time she touched one of them her hormones overrode her brain, and right now she needed to be thinking clearly.

Duncan inclined his head toward a doorway and then headed through it without another word. Tabi followed, ignoring the pain in her heel where she'd stomped on Jared's foot and the lingering weakness that still plagued her. As she entered the living room she had to refrain from goggling. The place was massive and looked like it had been taken stone by stone from a castle somewhere. Where the kitchen had been completely modern and sleek, this part of the house was completely different. Dark wood paneling lined the walls, and the windows were covered by heavy velvet drapes that were such a deep shade of burgundy they almost looked black until the firelight hit them. The fireplace was a massive and ornate affair, but she quickly realized that despite its ancient appearance it had to be a modern design, because the fire was gas-fed. There was even a heavy velvet curtain that could be pulled across the room, cutting it in half and creating a cozy area around the flickering flames. Tabi picked out a chair near the fireplace and settled herself into it, happy to be sitting down again. Whatever had happened to her out in the parking lot, the effects were certainly lingering.

As the others got settled, she watched, oddly disturbed by how at home Duncan looked surrounded by all these trappings of another time. With his long blond hair and leonine features, he seemed more warrior than healer at the moment. Duncan looked like he *belonged* here, and that thought set her to wondering if it was possible he really was as old as Jared had claimed. There was only one way to know.

"All right, Duncan, it's time for you to be honest with me. Are you really a three-hundred-year-old-vampire? And if so, what the hell are you doing working as a doctor?"

CHAPTER 4

THIS WAS what comes of bringing new people into one's life, Duncan thought to himself as he watched the firelight play over Tabi's lovely face. All it brought was chaos, confusion, and upheaval. No doubt that was exactly what the unknown vampire had intended by attacking Tabi and then leaving her alive. The vampire had known Duncan would have sensed their presence and come to investigate, and there was no way he could let a random stranger announce they'd been attacked by a someone who'd torn open their throat. The media would have had a field day and there would have been far too many questions. Though he had no doubt Tabi had been a random selection and not a carefully chosen target, Duncan couldn't help but think she was the best choice the other vampire could have made. He was already attracted to her, and now she was in his house, resistant to his charms and with an intact memory that he couldn't wipe. Her presence here was undoing decades of discipline and weakening his determination to keep his vow to never bring another into the darkness he lived in.

"Yes, I'm a vampire. I was born in Scotland three hundred and forty-seven years ago, though I haven't lived there in more than a century. And why shouldn't I be a doctor? It's a challenging line of work and it keeps me from going mad with boredom."

"But you—you're dead!"

Jared snickered and Duncan recalled the two of them having a similar conversation the night he'd made the younger man the offer to become his guardian. "No, I'm not."

"He's a bit dead," Jared chimed in helpfully.

"Dead is an inaccurate simplification. What I am is—"

"I swear, if you say it's complicated I'm going to start screaming again," Tabi interjected, her fingers tapping out an agitated rhythm on the arm of her chair.

"Very well, let's just say it's a bit of a mystery, and that's one of the reasons I'm a doctor. I've been trying to determine the science behind my condition. It's something of a hobby of mine." Tabi's lush lower lip vanished between her teeth as she considered his words and Duncan's mind filled with memories of the sweet taste of her mouth and the silken heat of her lips.

"Do you drink blood?" She finally asked it, the question he hated the most.

"Yes, but I don't kill anyone when I feed. I have never killed to feed, Tabitha. Not once." He'd killed for other reasons though, and Duncan could only hope she wouldn't press too far with her line of questioning.

"So you just attack and leave? Like what was done to me?" Her hand drifted up to her neck as she spoke, though he doubted she was even aware of what she was doing.

"No. I don't feed on the unwilling. What happened to you was an anomaly. Usually a vampire's victims don't even know they've been bitten."

"What do you mean, they don't know? They wake up with a hickey from hell and never wonder what happened?"

Duncan made a decision at that moment. He left his seat and crossed the room with enough supernatural speed to ensure Tabi had no chance to move before he had her caged, his hands curled around the arms of the chair she sat in, preventing escape. "I mean that there are usually only two ways vampires feed. Uncontrolled fledglings can go on a rampage fuelled purely by their appetites and they leave nothing but drained bodies and devastation in their wake. They rarely survive long, since without a creator to guide them they usually fall victim to accidents, violence or another vampire. We do not tolerate anything that could call attention to our existence." Duncan leaned in closer, enjoying the faintly fruity scent of her lotion, or perhaps it was her shampoo. "Vampires that survive the fledgling days learn to feed discreetly, using other methods."

"You mean you charm them into giving you what they want, just like you tried to do to me earlier."

"I don't normally need my abilities to charm a woman into my bed, Tabi. You've proven to be the exception to the rule."

"Bed? But I..." She trailed off, her mouth falling open as she stared up at him. "You sleep with the women you feed from? Don't you need to feed often? That's a lot of seduction."

"Feeding can be incredibly pleasurable, for both parties. I only charm them to remove the memory of what I did while we were together, and usually ensure they don't remember my name."

Tabi wrinkled her nose in distaste. "Oh, very classy. Wham, bam, thanks for dinner ma'am and off you go?"

Jared burst out laughing, whooping so hard he had trouble catching his breath as he doubled over in his chair. "She just pegged you bang on."

"It's mutually beneficial!" Duncan pushed in closer, until his mouth was only a finger's width from hers. "Usually I get what I need from bagged blood, if that makes you feel better. But when I hunt live prey, I'm very careful to be sure everyone gets what they want, and no one gets hurt."

"And you sneak out before the dawn, leaving her with the vampire version of a roofie and a fake phone number. Why did I ever think you were a nice guy?"

"Because you're attracted to me." He brushed his lips over hers. "And because I *am* a nice guy."

"No, you're a vampire," she murmured. Her lips moving against his and Duncan was pleased that she wasn't moving away from him. "And I'd say your seduction skills need work, because right now I'm sure as hell not interested in going to bed with you, no matter how incredible a kisser you are."

Duncan bit back a growl of frustration and rocked

back on his heels so that he was crouched at her feet. "I want you."

"I noticed. But since we've known each other more than a year and you've never so much as asked me out for coffee, I have to wonder what brought about this change of heart."

"I've always wanted you." He held her gaze and gathered one of her hands in his. "From the first time I saw you in the cafeteria. You had your head down and you looked so alone, and I remember thinking that a woman so beautiful shouldn't be sitting by herself."

"And yet you left me there, *alone*," Tabi pointed out.

"I did, but that was because I made a vow that I would never deliberately bring someone I cared about into the life I lead. I wanted you, but I didn't want to taint you with all *this*."

"So why now? If staying away from me was the right thing to do, why am I here?"

"You're here because whoever hurt you wanted to send me a message. They were looking to cause chaos and they did, even more than they could have known. By random chance they attacked the one person in that hospital that I cared about. When I caught your scent out in the parking lot and realized you were the one hurt..." He sighed and shrugged. "That's when I realized I hadn't been very smart in the way I'd been dealing with you."

"You mean your brilliant strategy to completely ignore me? Yeah, really not the best way to flatter a girl. The thing that attacked me, you knew it was out there?"

"Yes. We always know when another of our kind is nearby."

"Did you ever see that movie *Highlander* with Christopher Lambert?" Jared asked. "He's a bit like that. They can sense each other, and in the end, there can be only one in an area."

"So you kill each other?" Tabi's eyes widened again and Duncan was pleased to see a trace of concern for him present in her expression.

"I really hate that movie, Jared. I wish you'd stop quoting it so damned much!" He turned his attention back to Tabi. "My kind do not often have the need to go after each other, no. But we don't tolerate other vampires invading our territory, either. What this vampire has done is against all the rules we live by."

"Okay, so you knew it was out there, and they're making a point of messing up your life by leaving living witnesses and invading your territory. I think I have this so far. So why did you bring me here? I wasn't going to tell anyone I'd been attacked."

"I couldn't let you go back into the hospital with that injury, there would have been questions. I tried to wipe your memory, but your mind is too strong for that. So here we are. I never wanted this for you." He reached out to stroke her cheek, marveling at the softness of her skin. "But now that I have this chance, I can't say I'm sorry you're here."

"But I'm safe now, aren't I? The other vampire won't come after me again because I was just a random victim."

"I don't know. I hope so. But I would like you to stay here until I can be sure. Here you'll be safe." He stroked her cheek again. "And tonight we'll talk some more. I know you have the next few days off work, as do I. Stay with me." He glanced over at Jared. "Stay with us."

"So all it took to get your attention was to get attacked by a vampire?" She flashed him a faint smile and Duncan nearly roared with triumph at that faint sign of acceptance. "I'll stay, but only for today. Tonight we'll talk again and then I'll make my decision. I'm too tired to do any more thinking today."

"You need rest, and fluids." Duncan traced the line of her jaw to her ear and down her throat to where the gauze sat on her neck. "I would like your permission to heal this."

"I thought you already fixed it up?"

"I fixed it as a doctor. As a vampire, I have a more efficient method available to me."

"Then why didn't you do that the first time?" Tabi demanded, frowning now.

"If you had woken up without a mark on you despite remembering very clearly that you'd been attacked and hurt, do you think that would have helped matters?" He arched a brow up at her, pleased to see her spirit returning.

"I suppose not," she granted and then narrowed her gaze. "Just how exactly are you going to fix it?"

Jared chuckled. "Vampire blood has healing properties, which is another reason they're so very secretive about their existence. Imagine how interested the science geeks would be if they could get their hands on a source of instant healing remedies."

"You're going to *bleed* on me?" Tabi looked decidedly disgusted at the idea and Duncan burst out laughing.

"No, I'm going to kiss it better."

"That doesn't make any sense," she grumbled.

"Trust me, Tabi."

"Oh believe me, I do. If I didn't, you wouldn't be anywhere near me right now. Not unless I was tied to the chair."

"Interesting suggestion." Heat coursed through Duncan's body and his dick thickened and grew heavy at the image of Tabi naked and bound to the chair, her skin painted by firelight and the sweet taste of her pussy in his mouth. The vision was so vivid Duncan's fangs lengthened and his bloodlust spiked, responding to his deep arousal.

"Don't you even consider going there, fangs." Tabi's voice pulled him back to the here and now, and he curled his lip in distaste at her choice in nicknames. "I saw that look in your eye, and you can forget it. You haven't even bought me dinner yet."

"If I cook you dinner, does that count?" Jared asked. "I'll even throw in homemade cheesecake for dessert."

"You can make cheesecake?" Tabi turned away from Duncan to look at Jared and then back again. "Where did you find him, anyway? I know a lot of women who would kill to have a man like that."

"I'll tell you how I ended up with Duncan after you've slept," Jared promised. "He's not going to be around until sunset, we'll have plenty of time."

Duncan stood and moved around behind Tabi, his hands resting on the delicate bones of her shoulders. "Let me heal you before I retire."

She blew out a breath and nodded. "Okay."

He traced his fingers around the edge of the bandage, lifting it off as gently as he could. The flesh beneath was brutally torn and bruised, and Duncan swore that the vampire who had done this to his Tabi would be made to pay for every moment of pain she'd suffered. He buried his fingers into the rich, silken tumble of her hair and drew it away from her neck as he lowered his head and placed a kiss just above where the bruising ended. Tabi shivered and he caught the tiny gasp that escaped her lips. Her skin warmed beneath his mouth and he knew she was enjoying his touch.

Not wanting to push her newly found trust too far, Duncan let his fangs drop the rest of the way and then bit into his tongue until he could taste the blood in his mouth. He then delicately kissed his way over the wound, letting his blood heal her until there was not the slightest sign she had ever been injured at all.

When he finally lifted his head he could see the pulse point in her neck fluttering and the scent of strawberries mixed with the deeper, warmer scent of her blood. His fangs and cock both ached with the need to sink into Tabi's soft body and claim her for his own. Instead he pressed a kiss to the crown of her hair and then withdrew. He knew at that moment that his good intentions were all for naught. Tabitha Blacke was going to belong to him, mind, body, and soul. He wouldn't accept anything less.

TABI REACHED up to touch the newly healed area. She'd felt nothing but the delicious touch of Duncan's mouth on her skin and the faintest of chills, as if he'd held an ice cube in his mouth a moment before he'd kissed her. Now, her throat was healed, with not even a bruise or tender spot left where there'd been a mangled mess before. If she had needed more convincing that Duncan was what he claimed, that would have been enough. As it was, she'd already begun to accept that he was telling the truth. She wasn't sure how she felt about it all yet, but she believed him.

Duncan moved back to her side and leaned in close. With his eyes gleaming gold in the flickering light of the fire and his blonde hair framing his face, he looked more like a predator than ever, but she wasn't afraid. If he was going to hurt her, he would have. Tabi finally gave into months of yearning and ran her fingers through his hair. Duncan seemed almost startled by the intimate gesture and she nearly withdrew her hand, but then he leaned into her fingers, his lips nuzzling the inside of her wrist.

He stayed hovering over her, his mouth on her skin and her fingers buried in his hair until she made her choice and tugged him closer. When their lips met, his low, approving rumble filled her ears and she knew that somehow, somewhere in the past few seconds she'd made a choice to do more than simply believe him, she'd chosen to accept him despite the truth.

I'm clearly losing my mind.

His tongue traced the contours of her lips, a sensuous, delicate touch that made her clit tingle and swell. She tightened her grip on his hair and drew him in deeper. That was when her tongue brushed over one sharp, pointed fang and reality rushed in like a glacier-fed river, cooling her passion instantly. Her head snapped back and she gasped a single word like an accusation. "Fangs!"

Duncan straightened up and took a step back. "Sex and feeding are connected. And right now..."

"Right now if I had fangs they'd be showing, too," she confessed with a blush.

"If I have my way, you will have fangs one day, Tabi." Duncan turned to look at Jared. "Walk me to my chambers? We have things to discuss and very little time left."

Jared stood and Duncan turned his attention back to Tabi again. "Promise me you won't call anyone or try to leave this house."

Tabi opened her mouth to argue but then thought better of it. Besides, who would she call? No one would even notice she hadn't made it home. "I'll stay here, for now. But just so we're clear? A couple of hot kisses do not mean I'm good with fangs, vampires, or the whole blood drinking thing."

Duncan smiled, flashing his dimples as he leaned forward in a truncated bow. "We're clear. Sleep well, Tabi. I certainly know what I'll be dreaming about."

He gave her a slow wink and turned on his heel, leaving her gaping at his retreating back and an ass she was certain was damn near perfect. As Jared joined him, she took a moment to compare them and reflected that she was locked in a house with two of the hottest men she'd ever seen, and neither of them was normal. Well that at least she could accept. Her life had never been anything close to normal up to now, why break a trend?

Once she was alone Tabi leaned back in the chair and sighed. "Well this has been a seriously screwy day."

Although Duncan had fixed her neck, she was still stiff and bruised from being dropped into the snow, and her foot still hurt from her earlier escape attempt. At this point all she really wanted was some ibuprofen and for someone to wake her up and tell her it was all a dream. Yeah, that would be nice, but she knew it wasn't going to happen. She'd spent her entire childhood dealing with violence and darkness and things beyond her understanding, and not once had she had the luxury of waking up and finding out any part of it was a dream.

Her stepfather was a career criminal who still ran his empire from behind bars, and her stepbrothers were all as violent and cold as their father. The day her mother had died, Tabi had walked away from them all, changed her name and done everything she could to put distance between them. She'd even moved from New York to Chicago, leaving everything behind to start over again.

Tabi curled into the chair and closed her eyes before muttering to herself, "And now I'm crushing on a vampire *and* his minion and shacking up at his house because another vampire attacked me. Oh yes, I'd say this fresh start is going just brilliantly."

CHAPTER 5

JARED FELL in beside Duncan and the two of them walked in silence until they were well out of earshot of Tabi. Only then did Duncan halt and lean up against one side of the dimly lit hallway, looking straight at him. "You want her."

It was a statement, not a question, but Jared responded anyway. "Yes." There wasn't any point in denying it, not when they both knew the truth already. "And so do you."

"I do."

"So what are we going to do about this?" Jared leaned against the wall opposite Duncan and crossed his arms over his chest. "Flip a coin? Arm wrestle?" He decided to lay his cards on the table. "I know you've known her longer, but there's something about her that's going to make it hard for me to just let it go. I've been alone just as long as you have."

"I'm not going to let her go," Duncan declared. "She belongs here."

"I agree with you there, but that still leaves us with one question. Which one of us does she belong here with?"

"Perhaps she belongs with both of us." Duncan raised a brow. "If she agrees."

"Both of us?" Jared repeated, pleased and surprised at the suggestion. He'd hoped this might be possible, but he hadn't expected Duncan to consider it, at least not so quickly. "How are we even talking about this when you were growling 'mine' not long ago?"

Duncan smiled a slow, dangerous smile and Jared caught a glimpse of fang. "I didn't say it would be easy. We'd all have to work at it, but you and I both know this would be more in keeping with my true nature." He gave Jared an intent look. "You and I are closer than brothers already. If there was ever someone I could imagine sharing her with, it would be you." He paused and seemed to be choosing his next words with care. "To be honest I believe we'd have a better chance of keeping her here if she didn't have to choose between us. It's apparent she's attracted to us both." He reached up to touch the already healing scratches down his cheek. "It is also apparent that I misjudged her spirit. She is magnificent."

"She certainly is that." Jared let out a long breath and shook his head, bemused. "You think you know a guy, and then seventy-six years later, he surprises you." Images of Tabi, spread out and screaming in pleasure as the two of them enjoyed her together made Jared's cock hard and his balls tighten. Fuck yes, he could think of worse ways to spend eternity. "I've never considered the possibility of us sharing a woman. Hell, until tonight I never thought either of us would even consider dating again. Not after *her*."

"I never imagined I'd meet anyone who would make me consider rethinking my intentions to never turn another human. I certainly never considered the possibility we'd both want the same woman."

"But we do," Jared relaxed as he realized that this might actually work. That is if Tabi was willing to take them both on. *That* was going to take some salesmanship. Jared's thoughts darted here and there and another consideration struck him. "We've always kept the blood transfers between us impersonal. That was part of the agreement we made when I joined you. If Tabi stays, will you want to change that too?

Duncan's sensual smile turned downright wicked. "Are you saying you'd be willing to allow me to feed from you more intimately? I hadn't considered it, but if I have my way then Tabi will be feeding from you as well, and I suspect I'd enjoy seeing that very much. This shouldn't be an easy decision for any of us. If we do this. If she *is* willing, it will change everything."

Jared nodded his understanding. "Honestly? I think it's time for a change. But I'll give you my decision when you rejoin us tonight." Another vision flared in his head and Jared knew his grin was now as wicked as Duncan's. "I'll also give some consideration as to how to convince our guest to agree with what we're going to be proposing."

"That's not going to be easy either." Duncan stood

and glanced down the windowless corridor. "It's time for me to go. Keep her safe for us. I will see you after the sun sets."

Jared watched him go, knowing that Duncan preferred to be alone for the last few minutes before he succumbed to the lethargy that would already be stealing over his limbs, clouding his thoughts and rendering him weak and slow. It was the price every vampire paid for their existence, that when the sun rose, they became vulnerable. It was Jared's job to protect him while he slept.

When an electronic chirp indicated that Duncan had secured the door from within and was now safe for the day, Jared returned to the living room, ready to check up on his other charge. He found her dozing by the fireplace with one hand tucked under her cheek and her long legs drawn up so she was curled into the oversized chair like a kitten in a basket.

"C'mon, honey," he whispered in her ear. "It's time to tuck you in."

Her only response was a breathy little moan as she burrowed deeper into the chair.

"Stubborn woman. I swear, for a man who's been around three hundred years, Duncan doesn't know shit about judging a woman's temperament. Mousy, he said. All shy sweetness and sunshine." Jared snorted with laughter and then took the lobe of her ear into his mouth and nipped it very gently.

Tabi stirred and let out another little moan that had Jared's jeans feeling two sizes too small. If she decided to stay, either he'd be getting her naked as often as possible or he was going to need to buy bigger jeans.

"Jared?" She murmured in a voice thick with sleep. It pleased him no end that she hadn't thought it was Duncan waking her.

"It's me. It's time to go to bed."

"You woke me up to tell me to go to sleep?" Dark lashes fluttered open and she turned her head, moving her ear from his mouth as she did so.

"If you fall asleep down here you'll wake up all stiff and sore. We'll make a quick stop in the kitchen for water and ibuprofen, and then I'm putting you to bed."

"That's the best offer I've had in ages," she said and then blushed as she realized what she'd said. "Damn it, I meant bed sounds really good right now." She blushed brighter and ducked her head. "Shit, that wasn't what I meant either."

"I know what you meant." He curved a finger under her chin and tipped her head up so she was looking at him again. "But for the record, I'm game for taking you to bed anytime you say the word." Her lips parted slightly and that was all the invitation Jared needed. He held nothing back, letting her experience firsthand just how much she had affected him. She tasted of coffee, cream, and a sweetness that had nothing to do with sugar and everything to do with her own unique flavor. Jared teased her lips open with his tongue and sampled the soft heat of her mouth. When her hands curled into his sweater and pulled him in closer he didn't resist. As her breasts rubbed against his chest he could already imagine how it would feel when they were naked and pressed together, the way her legs would feel wrapped around his hips as he fucked her slow and deep.

She trembled beneath him and Jared lifted his head, worried he'd gone too far. When he looked down he found her watching him, her hazel eyes were bright with passion but also full of unease.

"What's the matter, honey?" He smoothed her hair back from her face and gave her a reassuring smile, but he kept his body pressed to hers. He liked having her beneath him.

"This isn't right. You. Me. Duncan." She blushed and she looked away from him again. "I'm not the type of person who does this."

"Me either, but this isn't something I think many people ever find. This is something special. I want you, Tabi. Though *want* doesn't exactly do justice to the way I'm feeling right now. "

"But... Duncan?"

"Duncan wants you too, and I can't blame him for that. I'm not going to blame you for that either."

She softened just a little and Jared knew he had her attention. "I've been with him for a very long time, an entire human lifetime in fact. We're closer than I ever imagined two people, especially two straight men, could ever be. Until you came along, I thought that was enough, but now?" He brushed a kiss to her cheek. "Now I know that we could be even better."

"Better how? This sounds complicated."

"It doesn't have to be. I'll explain it more when you wake up." Jared stood up and offered her his hand. "C'mon, it's nap time, little girl."

"You did not just say that!" She took his hand and stood, her eyes dancing with laughter and disbelief. "I'm a giant!"

Jared tugged her into his arms and kissed her as he laughed. "Compared to me you're not. Now stop being ornery and head to the kitchen."

"Ornery? Now I'm an ornery little girl?" She tossed her hair back over her shoulder and headed to the kitchen, doing her best to hide her limp.

"You certainly are. So how is it that Dr. Duncan thought you were a meek little mouse?"

"Oh, he was so busy staying away from temptation he only ever saw me in professional mode." Her smile faded as quickly as it had come. "He doesn't really know me at all."

"I think he does." Jared caught up to her and slid an arm around her slender waist. "If he didn't know you fairly well, he would never have brought you here. He knew you were strong enough to deal with the truth."

"But he said that it was because he couldn't take away the memory."

"He managed to get you to sleep, didn't he? Your mind is strong, but he could have forced it. He wanted a reason to bring you here." Jared winked. "Just don't tell him you're on to him. He probably believes his version of events. Let him have his delusions."

"You two lead a very odd life," Tabi observed as they reentered the kitchen.

"Not really, by vampire standards we're pretty boring. Duncan doesn't hunt often, he has a job, and we don't socialize with other vampires very much." He guided her to a chair and made her sit down before he grabbed the painkillers and cracked open a bottle of water for her.

"I've known for a while now that we needed a change. That Duncan needed to change the way he lived, but until now I've had no idea what that might entail. Now I think that you're going to be the catalyst for that change. You and this new threat."

"So other vampires think you two are *boring*? I'd hate to think what their lives must be like if having a job and not enjoying a steady diet of people makes you dull."

Jared handed her the ibuprofen and the water and laughed. "You need to remember that for most vampires sex and feeding are one and the same. It tends to color the way they think about the world. They're quite hedonistic by human standards." That was an understatement, but there'd be plenty of time to elaborate on that theme later.

"You said most vampires. And Duncan said he gets his blood from a bag most of the time. Why?" She washed down the pills and then yawned. "Sorry."

"I'll tell you anything you want to know, but not until you've slept."

"I'm too tired to even argue with you," she said and then threw back her head to down more than half the bottle of water. Jared stared at the long, elegant lines of her neck as she drank. She really was beautiful.

The moment she stood, he picked her up again, ignoring her protests as he carried her back to her bedroom. Finally she sighed and just rested her cheek against his chest in resignation. "I could have walked."

"You could have, but I know you're sore and tired, so why not let me take care of you?"

"Because nothing in this world comes without a price." Her answer was spoken with such absolute certainty that Jared knew she'd been taught that lesson young, and likely often. He was going to consider it a personal challenge to prove to her that wasn't always the case.

"Well the only price I plan on asking for is a good night kiss when I tuck you in. Think that's a fair deal?"

"Sold," she murmured, her voice already starting to thicken with exhaustion.

He backed into her room, using his hip to bump open the door so he could keep her in his arms just a little longer. Letting her go seemed like a bad idea, but he knew she needed to rest. While she was sleeping he was going to ramp up security around the house, ensuring that they'd be safe from anyone or anything that tried to come after them.

As he lowered her to the bed she smiled and ran her hands through his hair, drawing him down to give him a sweet, lingering kiss that had his dick straining at his jeans so hard he was certain the zipper was going to leave a permanent impression. Leaving her was a test of his willpower, but he finally broke the kiss and stood up, leaving her lying in the queen-sized bed alone. "Sleep well, mouse. The bathroom is through that door, and your clothes will be waiting for you."

"M'kay," she started to mumble and then her eyes flew open. "Did you just call me mouse?"

"Yep. It sorta suits you. Sweet dreams. I won't be far away if you need me."

He left her muttering under her breath, and he grinned as he closed her bedroom door. His vampire-blood enhanced senses were keen enough he could still hear every word she said even through the heavy wooden door. The mouse knew a few curses he'd never even heard before.

TABI CAME AWAKE WITH A SCREAM, her arms thrown up to ward off a blow that never came. Her heart was pounding and her body ached as if she'd spent hours at the gym and not at her desk at work. Before she could even remember what she'd been dreaming about her bedroom door burst open and two hundred pounds of muscle and heart-stopping hotness hurtled into the room and came to a stop at the foot of the bed.

"What is it? What's wrong?" he demanded and Tabi froze in shock.

Who the hell is that, and where the hell am I? This isn't my bedroom!

That was when her memories of the night before came rushing back and she was able to put a name to the stunning warrior-god standing in the middle of her bedroom, holding a shotgun in his hand.

"Jared?"

"You were screaming. Are you okay?" Jared scanned the entire perimeter of the room again before taking another step toward the bed. "Talk to me, honey."

"Nightmare," Tabi explained, still working on calming her heartbeat down to something close to normal.

Some of the tension left Jared's broad shoulders and he relaxed his grip on the gun. "Want to tell me about it, or would you rather I left you alone to go back to sleep? You've only been down seven hours or so."

Tabi didn't even think before she reacted, holding out her hand to him. "I don't want to be alone right now." Not when she could still hear the echoes of her screams in her mind and her throat still burned with the memory of the injuries she'd suffered at a monster's hands.

Jared nodded and circled around to the far side of the bed. He set the gun down on the floor with care before joining her. His much larger hand engulfed hers as he drew her into his arms and tucked her up against the comforting bulk of his body. "So, what was the nightmare about, the attack?"

"Yeah." Tabi snuggled into the sanctuary of his arms and closed her eyes as she tried to recall what she could. "Only it was more like a memory than a dream. I know for sure it was a man now, it was a man with dark hair and cold hands."

Jared's arm tightened around her and she felt a faint rumble of displeasure roll through him. "I'm sorry you had to go through that."

"Well, I didn't have you around to protect me then." The words were out of her mouth before Tabi could edit herself. "I mean..."

"You're right, you didn't. But I'm here now, and I won't let anything happen to you."

Jared's words unlocked a part of her heart Tabi had thought she'd sealed away forever. Hope and the beginnings of trust flooded her heart and it was almost painful to let it happen, but she did. She held tight to his hand and forced herself to take his words into her soul.

"Do you mean that?" Her voice was barely louder than a breath, but somehow he heard her anyway.

"I meant every word. It doesn't matter if you are mine, Duncan's, both of ours, or neither of ours. Whatever happens, I'll be there if you need me. I promise."

The pain in her heart receded, washed away by a sparkling fountain of joy. "I never imagined my guardian angel would have a Texas drawl."

"You're one of the blessed ones." He laughed and the vibration traveled through her, spurring her to join in. When they were both quiet again he asked, "Do you remember anything else?"

"Only bits and pieces, but he said something just before I lost consciousness. He leaned in close and whispered it."

"What did he say?"

"He said to relay a message to the one who found me. He told me to tell them that Ruth's revenge was coming soon." Tabi tipped her head up so she could look into Jared's face. "Do you have any idea what he was talking about?"

"You're sure he said the name Ruth?" Jared's voice had an edge to it now.

"I'm sure." Tabi bit her lip and sighed. "That's not a good thing, is it?"

"No, it's not. But at least now we know what this is

about." He blew out a breath and dropped a kiss to her temple. "He didn't do anything else to you, did he?"

"Anything else?" It took Tabi a second to understand what he meant. "Uh, no. I mean, I don't think so. I don't remember anything after that, and I woke up in the snow only a few minutes later. He didn't have time to do anything else apart from use me for an appetizer."

"Good. Then maybe we'll let him die quickly," Jared muttered and Tabi winced at his dark words that invoked memories of other men and other violence.

"You're going to kill him?"

"I don't think we're going to have much choice. He's the one that started this. Does that bother you?"

"A little," Tabi admitted.

"He's already attacked you, and he's going to keep attacking others until he gets what he wants. Innocent people are going to get hurt, maybe even killed. Duncan and I are going to have to stop him and Ruth."

"I've heard statements like that my whole life. There's always a justification for violence, or even for killing if someone wants to do it badly enough. That doesn't make it right." Tabi sighed. "But I suppose this isn't something we can just go to the police over either."

"Not unless they have a supernatural investigation unit I'm not aware of. This part of Chicago is Duncan's territory. It's not just his hunting ground, it's his home, and he's expected to protect it and its occupants from other vampires. It's all part of the rules they exist by. No one else is supposed to hunt here without permission. It's a courtesy thing most of the time, but when something like this happens, he's expected to deal with it."

Tabi absorbed that bit of information in silence, finally deciding it was something she was going to have to accept if she decided to stay. One problem at a time, she reminded herself before breaking the silence with a question. "So, can you tell me who Ruth is?"

"I'll tell you who she *was*, and how I came to meet Duncan, if you promise to tell me who it was that taught you that there's always a justification for violence."

"I suppose the two of you have trusted me with enough of your secrets that I shouldn't be worried about telling you mine." She laughed into the soft wool of his sweater. "By comparison, my secrets are quite tame."

"I don't think there's a whole lot about you that's tame, to be honest. But you just go on pretending if that's what you want to do."

"I'm not pretending!" Tabi lifted her head to argue and found herself flipped onto her back and pinned to the mattress. Her mouth was sealed against Jared's as he loomed over her, his hands splayed on either side of her shoulders. "Tabi." Jared groaned her name as he rocked his hips against her pussy, letting her feel the steel-hard shaft of his cock as he pressed it to the seam of her cunt.

She opened her mouth to his and moaned as his tongue slipped inside and tangled with hers, tasting and teasing her until her skin felt like fire and her blood was roaring in her ears. She reached for him, her fingers stroking over the powerful width of his shoulders as she drew him down and deepened their kiss.

Tabi was burning up from the inside out, and every second Jared kissed her she only got hotter. Need flared deep in her womb and she felt her pussy getting wetter and slicker with each kiss. Her response to Jared was so intense it bordered on terrifying, and until last night she'd never experienced anything even close to it.

And now I'm getting hot and bothered by not one, but two gorgeous men. Maybe that attack in the parking lot put me in a coma, and this is all a really, really vivid dream.

That thought gave her the giggles and soon Jared pushed himself up and off her just enough to give her a crooked grin, his green-gray eyes twinkling with amusement. "And what, pray tell, is so damned funny?"

"I was just thinking that if this is a dream, I never want to wake up. Vampires are real, I'm a guest in the home of a man I've had a crush on for more than a year, and now his very hot guardian is in bed with me. This is the strangest, and possibly the best dream I've ever had."

"It's no dream, honey. You're really here, and we're both hoping that eventually you'll agree to stay with us."

"You can't mean that. Neither of you can. Especially not when forever has a very different connotation for two men who are more or less immortal."

Jared shrugged and the muscles under her hands rippled and flowed with the movement. "I don't say anything I don't mean. I knew I would accept Duncan's offer within a few hours of meeting him, and I've never regretted that decision. I have the same feeling when it comes to you. You're supposed to be here."

He lowered his body back over her and kissed her again, his mouth gentler this time. When she tried to pull him down though, he eased away from her and settled back down on his side of the bed. "One thing I've learned since I started to work for Duncan is that there's a force at work in the world. It puts people where they are supposed to be, when they're supposed to be there. Sometimes folks don't see it and they miss out, but that doesn't mean that they weren't ever given the chance. You've got a chance here, mouse, but no one can make you decide to take it."

"You're not going to stop calling me that ridiculous nickname, are you?" Tabi sighed in mock frustration, trying to lighten the mood and evade the pointed look Jared was giving her.

"Nope. It's staying. Hopefully I'll be calling you that for a very long time." He grinned. "You might even get to like it, given a decade or three."

With that Jared reached for her again, drawing her back into his arms so that her back was pressed to his chest and his arm was curved around her waist. She could feel his breath fanning her hair, and his voice was a warm rumble near her ear. "Do you want me to tell you who Ruth is now?"

"Yes, please. It would be nice to know the meaning behind the message I was used to deliver."

"All right then, but be warned that there are going to be some parts of this story you may not want to hear. Just keep in mind this all happened long before you were even born."

"Ancient history, got it," Tabi quipped, but she wondered what Jared was about to tell her, and if she'd been smarter to just leave well enough alone.

"Ruth was Duncan's last guardian. He fell for her, changed her into a vampire, and then discovered that he'd made a terrible mistake. That was when he found me and offered me the job as his guardian. We spent the next few years tracking her down and putting things to right again."

Tabi felt her stomach turn over and she had to swallow before she could ask her next question. "So when that man talked about Ruth's revenge, what did he mean?"

"It means that something's gone very wrong. Duncan believed he killed Ruth a long time ago. The rules they live by are very clear on such things. A fledgling vampire is the responsibility of the one who made them, and Ruth was a rogue, completely out of control. Duncan had no other choice."

"So who's out for revenge if she's dead?"

"I don't know, and that's the part that worries me."

CHAPTER 6

WHEN THEY'D FINISHED TALKING, Jared left Tabi to enjoy a long soak in a bathtub so big she'd declared it a swimming pool and went down to the kitchen to start working on dinner. Cooking relaxed him and helped him think, and right now he needed to be calm and clearheaded.

Hearing about Tabi's criminal stepfather and siblings had left him angry and hurting for the girl she'd been, and had given him a lot of insight into the woman she'd become. He'd meant what he'd said to her about fate putting people where they needed to be, and after learning about Tabi's past, Jared had no doubts at all that she had been destined to become part of their lives. She was a lot like he'd been when Duncan had found him. Wandering through life, trying to find a place to fit in and people to care about. When Duncan had refused to acknowledge his attraction to his coworker, fate had simply upped the ante and dropped her directly into Duncan's path. It was one of the least subtle machinations Jared had seen in his life, and he for one was more than happy to take what was being offered without further argument. He just hoped that Tabi and Duncan were going to be as easygoing about it. Somehow, he doubted that.

He had the steaks marinating and the cheesecake almost defrosted by the time she came downstairs to join him, her hair loose and still damp from her bath and her skin soft and pink from the heat of the water.

"Hey, mouse. Coffee?"

"Please." She smiled at him and took a seat at the table while he poured her a mug and set it down in front of her. She looked younger with her hair tumbled around her face, and his fingers itched to bury themselves in those dark waves and then work their way slowly lower, until he'd explored every inch of her gorgeous body all the way down to her toes. He was pleased to see she'd worn the clothes he'd left out for her instead of what had been salvaged from her work wardrobe.

He liked seeing her in his clothes. Her long legs were covered in a fresh pair of his track pants with the drawstrings cinched in over her slender hips and she'd picked out another of Duncan's sweaters with the cuffs rolled halfway up her forearms. He wanted to slide a hand under those pants and find out if she'd gone commando or taken his unspoken dare and worn the men's briefs he'd left out for her too. The thought of her wearing his underwear had Jared instantly hard, and he realized that his little game had backfired.

As if reading his thoughts Tabi raised her gaze to his and gave him a wink, and he nearly groaned as a fresh surge of blood hit his dick and made it swell painfully tight behind the zipper of his jeans. Yeah, he was in trouble, big time.

"How are you feeling?" he asked as he finished the preparations and brought his half-empty mug of coffee over to the table to join her.

"A little tired, but not bad all things considered. The bath helped, I just wish I had some of my own things to wear." She touched her face absently. "And makeup would be nice. I hardly recognized myself in the mirror without it."

"You look beautiful. More like the women of my time, to be honest. I never really got used to all the cosmetics and potions you ladies have started using." He reached out to stroke her cheek and then brushed a lock of her hair back behind her ear. "You could bring some things here, you know. Or get Duncan to buy you a whole new wardrobe. Do you have any idea how much money you can make when you have centuries to get a return on your investment? It's obscene."

"I couldn't ask him to do that, I don't want anyone's charity."

"It wouldn't be charity. Think of it this way. He's the one charged with protecting the people of this town from vampire attacks. You were attacked by a vampire anyway. He failed to protect you, therefore, he owes you. At the very least he owes you a new outfit to replace the one that got trashed last night."

Duncan joined in the conversation, startling Tabi. "Indeed I do. Though I'm not sure I appreciate the fact that you just described me as a failure."

"Sorry, boss. I'm just calling it as I see it. She *did* get bitten." Jared grinned at Duncan. "You're up earlier than I expected, sunset isn't for what, another hour?"

"Wait a second, if the sun is up, how are you awake? Aren't you supposed to be tucked away in a sun-proof vault somewhere waiting for nightfall?" Tabi looked perplexed as she looked at Duncan and then out the window at the gray daylight.

"More Hollywood misconceptions I'm afraid. I am weakest when the sun rises, and then my strength slowly returns as the sun travels toward sunset. I do not crawl into a coffin and go catatonic during the day however. I simply sleep in a secure location."

"So sunlight doesn't make you turn to dust or burn you?"

"I'm old enough that the sun doesn't bother me very much any longer, but I certainly don't tan either."

"So no dust, but no sparkles?" Tabi asked and Jared caught the impish gleam in her eyes.

"No." Duncan ground out the syllable from between clenched teeth, his brogue thickening. "I do *not* fucking well sparkle!"

"Careful, mouse. He ate the last person who asked him that," Jared warned, choking back laughter.

"Mouse?" Duncan arched a brow and looked at Jared as Tabi growled in frustration.

"Mouse, as in mousy. It's your fault he's tagged me with that ridiculous nickname, fangs."

"Fangs? Mouse? What's with all the nicknames?" Duncan grumbled and poured himself a cup of coffee while Tabi gawked.

"Yeah, I got him hooked on coffee. It helps give him a boost when he gets up early." Jared saved Duncan from another explanation and leaned back in his chair. "And the nicknames weren't planned, they just sort of happened."

"Well make them stop happening."

Jared turned at winked at Tabi. "Did I mention he's really cranky when he first wakes up? Don't worry, it doesn't last long."

"Only as long as it takes me to fire my manservant," Duncan muttered and Jared threw up his hands in surrender. "I'll be good. Just don't call me that."

"Manservant?" Tabi commented, grinning. "Huh, and here I thought you were the butler."

They kept the banter up all through dinner, and for once it was a cheerful meal that had laughter echoing off the walls of the kitchen and filling the house with something it had always been missing: a sense of family.

TABI STILL WASN'T sure how they'd managed to convince her to stay with them for a few more days, but as she opened the door to her cramped and sparsely furnished apartment she had to admit that it probably had something to do with the fact her bed at Duncan's was bigger than her entire bedroom here. That and the fact that her place was decidedly short on sexy, protective hunks that had made it very clear that they wanted her safely under their protection. Not to mention under them, singly or together. She wasn't ready to agree to that last bit yet, but there was no point in denying the fact she was attracted to them enough to at least consider it.

Duncan had swung by the hospital and they'd picked up her car before driving over to her place to pick up a few things. She unlocked her apartment door and was halfway down the cramped hallway before she realized that Duncan hadn't come in yet. As she turned around she spotted the look of frustration on his face and she had to squelch the urge to laugh. "You're kidding me, right? You actually can't come in without an invitation?"

"Stop laughing and let me in, Tabi. It's not funny."

"Oh, I beg to differ. The expression on your face right now is priceless." She leaned up against the wall and raised a brow at him. "What's it worth to you?"

Duncan's eyes flared brilliant gold and he snarled under his breath before answering her. "Tabitha Amy Blacke. Invite me in right now or so help me..."

"You really are a lot of fun to tease, has anyone told you that before?" Being back in her own home again had given Tabi back some of her equilibrium, and she was finally able to enjoy flirting with Duncan now that he didn't hold all the cards. Feeling more than a little brazen, she licked her lips and then tweaked the sleeve of her borrowed sweater. "I'm considering leaving you there while I go change out of your clothes and back into mine."

He leaned into the empty air, frustration making his eyes blaze as he tried to push through whatever invisible force blocked the doorway. "Tabi. Let. Me. In."

"If I do, you have to tell me how you know my middle name."

"Fine."

"Come in, Duncan. Make yourself at ho—"

He was on her before she could finish her sentence. He growled as his powerful body pressed against hers from knee to chest and his hands framed her face, tipping her head up as he kissed her with savage intensity. His mouth raked across hers and she felt the sharp point of a fang slide across her lower lip. Tabi gasped and Duncan pressed in closer, plunging his tongue into her mouth to duel with hers as his hands left her face to close around her hips. She felt herself being lifted, her feet dangling in the air as Duncan slid her up the wall, insinuating his thigh between her legs and grinding his cock against her with another possessive growl.

Need coursed like quicksilver through Tabi's veins and she reacted without thinking. She wrapped her legs around his waist as her arms looped around his neck, capturing him just as surely as he had captured her. Duncan released her hips and slid his hands under her sweater, his fingers finding her breasts with unerring swiftness. He held them in his palms, fingers tweaking and pinching at her nipples until they rose up into taut peaks. Every touch sent a bolt of heat straight to her pussy and Tabi moaned and arched herself harder against the rigid shaft of his cock. Her clit was swollen now and every touch of Duncan's hands was making her ache with the need to be touched.

Duncan lifted his head and Tabi gasped for breath to fill her nearly empty lungs. Before she could gather her scattered thoughts he uttered her name like it was an invitation to pleasure itself and pressed another kiss to her mouth. Something tugged at the back of her mind and she fought against the temptation to lose herself in his kiss and the flames of passion that were heating them both from the inside out. There was something...

"Door!" she exclaimed as she finally realized what was wrong. They'd left the damned door to her apartment wide open.

Duncan chuckled. The sound reverberating through them both as he turned his head and she watched in shock as the door slammed shut hard enough to make the wood shimmy in its frame. "Anything else?"

"How'd you do that?"

"I'm an old vampire. I can do all sorts of things." The sultry tone in his voice made Tabi's pussy gush. "I want to show you all of them." His fingertips teased at her nipples again, sending sparks of desire sizzling over her skin. "You wanted to know how I knew your full name. It's because I know everything there is to know about you, Tabi. At least I thought I did. I know your real name and who your family is. I know you prefer your coffee black but like honey in your tea. I know so many facts about you, but I never got to know the woman behind the facts. I want to make that up to you. Don't ever put a door between us again Tabi, or I swear to the gods I will tear the house down around you. I don't intend to ever be separated from you again."

Her head was reeling and her heart was caught somewhere between joy and terror at his words. "Why?" was the only word to tumble out of her mouth from the myriad whirling inside her mind.

"Why?" Duncan parroted her. His voice was rough

and his hands were still working her breasts with clever flicks of his fingers. "Because I haven't felt anything for anyone in a very long time and yet the moment I saw you, I knew you could change all that. I want you like I haven't wanted a woman in centuries. I'm done fighting with destiny. I know where I'm supposed to be, and who I'm supposed to be with."

"What if I don't know that yet?" Tabi demanded as old fears reared up and filled her heart and soul with remembered pain. "What if you're not what *I* want?"

"You don't have to be certain yet, but you can't try and tell me that you don't want me. Not when your legs are wrapped around my waist and I can taste you on my tongue." He drew his mouth across hers to make his point. "Stay with me for a few days. Stay with us, Tabi. Let us keep you safe and get to know each other."

"I already agreed to that," she whispered, her lips moving against his as she buried her hands in his long blond hair.

"Then say yes again. Say yes to all of it."

The words caught in her throat and tears pricked at her eyes as Tabi fought a brief but silent war with her past. When she finally made her decision, her acceptance was a barely heard murmur against his cheek. "Yes. I don't know why I trust you, but I do. Both of you. So my answer is yes."

With that whispered surrender still hanging in the air between them Duncan's mouth sealed over hers, kissing her past thought and reason until nothing existed but his touch and the powerful demands his body was making of hers. His hands turned and she felt the sweater she was wearing tear, the yarn shredding like paper. He left it hanging over her skin in tatters as his hands returned to her hips, lifting her higher as he released her lips and lowered his head so that his lips brushed over one berry-red nipple, teasing it with a lash of his tongue before he sucked it deep into the heat of his mouth.

Tabi cried out at the raw pleasure of his touch, her hips rocking as she ground herself down hard on the throbbing length of his cock where it lay trapped behind denim and the metal of his zipper.

She tugged on his hair and was rewarded with a rasping grunt of approval that vibrated around her sensitized nipple and drew another moan from her throat.

He moved to suckle at her other breast and again she felt the brush of a fang against her skin, the point so sharp it felt as though the slightest pressure could cause it to pierce her flesh. An image of Duncan biting her and latching onto her breast to feed filled her head and her pussy clenched in response to the erotic thought. She was so wet she could feel her thighs growing slick as she rubbed herself along Duncan's marble-hard cock again and again.

Finally he tore his mouth from her breast and she looked into his eyes, seeing the golden glow flaring deep in their depths as he reached back and unwound her legs from his hips and kissed her as he slowly lowered her back to her feet. Before she could do more than untangle her fingers from his hair he was helping her get free of the ruined tatters of what had once been his sweater, drawing it up over her head and tossing it aside with an impatient flick of his wrist.

"Let me see you," he ordered, drawing her hands back away from her breasts, which she had instinctively covered. "I've imagined this moment often enough, I want to know if I got the details right." He smiled and her stomach flip-flopped as his dimples flashed and a curve of fang appeared for a moment at the corner of his mouth.

His eyes devoured her and he finally seemed satisfied. "I never imagined you were quite so perfect."

Tabi grinned and blushed at the same time. "I want to see if I got the details right, too. I just never imagined I'd get the chance to find out."

Duncan went still and arched one blond brow. "What did you imagine we were doing?"

She blushed deeper and shook her head. Why'd she say anything? There was no way she could tell him all the fantasies he'd starred in since she'd first seen him at the hospital. Could she?

He skinned his sweater over his head and all the air whooshed out of Tabi's lungs as she saw him bare-chested for the first time. Not even on her best day had she imagined him to be so well built. Broad shoulders tapered down to a trim waist, and there wasn't an inch of him that wasn't toned and sculpted. Unable to resist, she ran her fingers through the pale-gold hairs that covered his chest and marked the path downward over a perfect set of abs to vanish beneath the waistband of his jeans. She followed the trail down to his fly, letting her fingers brush over the button on his jeans. Duncan's breath caught and she liked knowing that her touch could affect him.

"Don't stop now." His voice was low and she could hear the hunger in it. "Tell me what you dreamed I'd do to you, Tabi." His hands covered hers and he bucked his hips in encouragement.

She wet her lips with the tip of her tongue and took a shaky breath as she undid his jeans, taking her time to explore the impressive length of his cock as she eased the zipper down an inch at a time. "Every time I used the back stairs I'd imagine the two of us meeting there. You wouldn't speak, not even to say my name, but you would pull me into your arms and kiss me until I was dizzy. Then you'd bend me over the railing and fuck me right there in the stairwell."

"The back stairs, huh?" Duncan's dick twitched at her words and she let her hand slip inside his jeans. Her fingers curled around the thick width of his cock and a fresh coating of honey slickened her pussy lips as she realized he was bigger than she'd imagined. Lurid thoughts of how it would feel to have him pounding into her body and stretching her to her limits were inter-rupted by Duncan's next query.

"Did I make you scream? Did you like having my cock inside you?"

His words flowed over her like dark honey and Tabi moaned as her cunt tightened and pulsed between her thighs. "Every night when I used my vibrator I imagined it was your cock inside me, your hands making me feel good," she confessed and the words made her hotter, her wicked admission setting free a part of her personality she had never explored.

"Tell me what you imagined us doing, lass." Duncan's

brogue was back and his lips were brushing over the curve of her ear and down her throat in tiny nibbles as he slid the track pants down over her hips and bared her to the knee. "Did I fuck you hard, or make you beg me for every inch I gave you?"

"Hard." She caressed the length of his cock and he groaned in response. "So hard I could barely stand up afterward."

"Do you want me to fuck you like that now, Tabi?" His breath fanned over her skin and she was finding it hard to catch her breath as reality and her fantasies collided. Duncan was here, offering to do everything she'd always dreamed of.

"Yes. Oh god yes I want that."

"Then that's what we'll do." He gently moved her hand off his cock and then dropped to his knees on her threadbare carpet, dragging her pants down to her ankles as he nuzzled his face between her thighs, his tongue tracing the seam of her pussy. He grasped her ankle and tugged it free of the fabric before guiding her leg up over his shoulder so she was slightly off balance and feeling very exposed. Golden eyes met hers and he grinned, his canine teeth clearly visible now. "Wicked girl, not wearing any underwear. Best you lean back and hang on, I'm about to make both our fantasies come true."

Tabi whimpered as anticipation blended with a need so strong she couldn't think straight any longer. She tangled one hand into his hair and splayed one against the wall behind her, a cry tearing from her throat as Duncan used his thumbs to spread her labia wide and blew a stream of warm air over her swollen clit.

"Sweet. Wet. Mine," he rumbled before nuzzling deeper between her thighs and letting his tongue go to work on her clit, flicking at the tiny pearl until she was quivering.

"Let me come now," she pleaded.

"No." The single word was snarled back at her as he drew her clit into his mouth and eased two fingers into her pussy. The extra stimulation had Tabi on the verge of orgasm, but he held her there, moving too slowly to push her over the edge. His long fingers pumped in and out and he kept her clit captive under his tongue, pushing her to the point of mindless begging.

"Fuck, let me come. Please, Duncan. I need...I want... I...I..." She babbled, broken and needy, and still he drew out the pleasure until her legs were quaking and her begging had become a hoarse whisper of "please," repeated time and again.

That was when he finally let her go over the falls and into the churning waters of an orgasm that tore her world apart and sent her spinning into mindless darkness. His fingertips brushed over some secret spot far inside her just as his teeth closed lightly on her clitoris and she shattered into pieces, coming so hard she slid down the wall and crumpled to the floor, still crying out in pleasure.

CHAPTER 7

BEING with Tabi was even more incredible than he'd imagined. She was so responsive to his touch and her passion was a glorious thing to watch as she came undone above him. Duncan's fantasies had been nothing compared to having Tabi in his arms for real, and he would never forgive himself for the loss of all the nights he could have been enjoying the sweet taste of her mouth and the sound of her screaming his name in rapture.

As she slumped to the floor he followed her down, only pausing long enough to shed his jeans before covering her body with his. Gods above and below, he needed this woman. She greeted him with a hungry kiss that had him groaning into her open mouth as her limbs wrapped around him and drew him in closer. The long legs that had filled his dreams for months were finally snug around his hips and his cock was poised just outside the slick opening to her pussy.

"Duncan." Her soft voice whispered his name and he

found himself staring into the green and gold depths of her eyes, amazed to find more than need there. More than just desire, there was a glimmer of trust, and even fainter there was a trace of something that made his heart pound a little harder. This beautiful woman cared for him.

"You're mine, Tabitha." He claimed her body with one slow and steady thrust that didn't end until he was completely encased in the tight sheath of her body. The walls of her pussy gripped and pulsed around his cock and he had to remind himself that this time he would not feed. This night he would make love to his woman as a man. The vampire would have to wait.

Beneath him Tabi arched up, taking him deeper still until his balls were touching the wet heat of her cunt. "Fuck me, Duncan." She breathed against his lips before kissing him again.

There was no charm here, no artificially ramped up desire. Her need kindled a forest fire of lust in Duncan's ancient heart and he let himself go. His hips arched up and then pressed back down hard enough to pin her to the floor with a soft thump as her ass hit the threadbare carpets. He straightened his arms to raise himself above her and watched her face as he pumped his cock deeper into her body with more force than he would normally allow himself. This time was different. This was his woman, and he wanted her to feel him. He needed her to feel his strength and know he'd use it to protect her, he wanted to mark her forever as his and then shelter her from a world he knew had been cruel to her. He fucked her harder, pounding into her in a frenzy as she gasped and mewled beneath him. Her nails clawed across his shoulders, biting into his flesh with a burning sting that only made the fire of his lust burn hotter.

His hands were braced above her shoulders, keeping her body from moving along the floor. He kissed her hard and tasted blood and knew that he'd not been careful enough with his fangs. That single taste of her life essence threatened to unleash the darkness he'd been determined to hold back, and he threw back his head with a snarl of frustration.

"No," he growled. "I won't."

The hand that had clawed him only a second before reached up to stroke his cheek and Duncan glanced down at Tabi and was amazed by the complete trust he saw there. "You won't, because you know I'm not ready yet." She tangled her fingers into his hair and drew him down to kiss him, ignoring his fangs. She soothed his blood hunger with nothing more than a touch and an act of trust.

Incredible.

He slowed his strokes, arching his body to make sure her clit was caressed with every thrust. His tongue danced and darted with hers, echoing the joining of their bodies as he began to near the end of his control. She fit him so tightly it bordered on painful each time she gripped his cock with her inner muscles, and he shifted his weight so that he was supported on one arm as he reached between them to pinch and tease her swollen clitoris until he felt her quaking on the edge of another orgasm. Only then did he drive them both over the edge, coming hard as she cried out again and bucked beneath him. His world exploded into sensations, noise, and pleasure as he emptied himself into her womb in a continuous stream of cum that had him breathless and unable to think by the time it was done.

Her release still had her pussy fluttering and pulsing around his dick and he lingered inside her body instead of withdrawing immediately as he had always done before. This was Tabi and that meant that everything was different. The thought should have concerned him, but it didn't. He was more than ready for the changes she was going to make in his world. He thought about Jared and smiled to himself. She was bringing changes to both of them.

"I'd say by that smile you enjoyed that almost as much as I did." Tabi's voice brought him back from his musings and he dropped a kiss to her sweet lips.

"Enjoy isn't strong enough a word. I loved it." He nipped her earlobe next and groaned as her pussy gripped his cock in response. "And I'm going to love doing that to you again as soon as we get up off this floor and you point me the way to your bedroom."

"Again?" Tabi moaned and then grinned. "Vampires are sexy, hot, and have great stamina, too? How did I not know this?"

"Because we take very good care to keep our existence a secret," Duncan told her, laughing as he withdrew from her body before gathering her into his arms and standing.

"It's too bad they're also really slow to ask a girl out." She stuck her tongue out at him. "Think of all the incredible sex we've been missing out on."

"Oh believe me, I'm already regretting it. You'll never know how much."

"Good." She looked up at him with a sweet smile that warmed his soul. "I'm willing to try and make up for lost time if you are."

"That's my intention, lover. Now you're in my arms, I have no intention of letting you go again." He paused, staring at two identical doorways. "Which way?"

"Bathroom on the left, bedroom on the right."

He swung to the right and managed to get the door open while still holding Tabi in his arms, revealing a cramped space with a smallish bed and an old battered dresser.

"Sorry, it's not much." Tabi started to squirm in his arms and he felt her growing tension and realized it was because she was embarrassed for him to see how little she had.

"I do not judge a person on their possessions." He kissed her, savoring the sweet flavor of her mouth. "Besides, you're coming to live with me now, so what does it matter what you had, or didn't have? We'll have what you want packed up and brought over, and the rest can be donated to someone who needs it." Duncan lowered her gently to the bed, noting that the mattress was old and sagged in several places as he stretched out beside her.

"Will you let us take care of you? You deserve so much more than you've been given in life."

"How much do you know?" Tabi snuggled into him and reached for a handmade quilt, laying it over them both.

"All of it. Your stepfather and his criminal activities,

the police reports your mother refused to sign, the social worker you were too afraid to talk to. I read about it all."

"I don't want to know how you found all that. No one at work knows. The youth files are sealed, and I did everything I could to distance myself from it all. I even changed my last name."

"I have been around a long time, I know a few tricks. Not to mention the fact that Jared and I have both had to change our identities from time to time."

"So your name's not Duncan Masterson?" She sat up a little, looking unhappy at the idea he'd changed his name.

"Actually, it is. I'd not used that name in more than a hundred years, so when I arranged to come to Chicago, I decided to come as myself."

"And Jared?" She pressed and it pleased Duncan to know that it mattered to her.

"Jared's last name used to be something else. Evan was his father's name. So when the time came for a change, Evans seemed a good choice."

"That makes sense." Tabi laughed suddenly. "I just realized, we've all changed our names and hidden our pasts at one point or another. Funny how we've got that in common."

"I don't think it's funny at all. I think it's fate. You're meant to be with us. Jared and I. We need you."

"That's a lovely sentiment, but—"

Duncan cut her off by pressing a finger to her lush lips, still reddened and swollen from their kisses. "But nothing. You don't live as long as I have without seeing destiny in action. You were always supposed to be part of my life. I was just fighting the inevitable."

"That's what Jared said, too. You really believe in fate?"

Duncan wrapped her in his arms and drew her in closer. "I really believe in us," he told her before giving in to the need to kiss her again.

IT HAD TAKEN Tabi a pathetically short amount of time to pack the few things she truly needed or wanted. The sum of her existence now rested in a battered suitcase sitting in the trunk of Duncan's car. Somehow things had changed in the hours that she and Duncan had spent making love and talking. She'd gone back to her place to get the few things she would need for a short stay, but when she had walked out of her apartment, it was with the sense she would never be back again. She'd even packed her family photo album. It contained the treasured glimpses of the brief flashes of happiness that had shone brightly in an otherwise dark and lonely childhood.

Duncan hadn't needed to use his vampire charms to convince her to move in with them. All he'd had to do was talk to her and show her a little bit of the man he was behind the mask he wore, and she'd agreed without so much as a moment's doubt. At least there hadn't been any doubts while she was packing. That had changed the moment she'd gotten into the car. Since then, doubts had assailed her every second of the drive back to what was now, for all intents and purposes, her home.

"You're thinking too much," Duncan glanced over at her, his amber eyes gleaming with intelligence and something more.

"And you're hungry," Tabi responded.

"How'd you know?" Duncan blinked in surprise at her assessment.

"Your eyes. They're glowing a little. How often do you need to feed?"

"Just like you, I need about three meals a day. The difference is my meals happen to be in liquid form." He winked at her. "And just like you, I get hungrier after I've exerted myself. Right now I am famished."

Tabi blushed at the memory of all the wicked, sensual things they'd done to earn their appetites. "I'm a bit hungry myself," she confessed.

"If I know Jared, he'll have left us both a snack in the kitchen. We'll eat and then you and I can talk a bit more about what it means to be part of my life." He placed a possessive hand on her thigh, his thumb stroking in slow circles over the top of her knee. "There are a few things we need to go over, and I'm sure you'll have questions. Then you should get some sleep. I know it isn't easy for you, trying to spend time with both Jared and me when we keep such different hours. I have a few thoughts on how we can make that easier."

"You're really all right with the idea of my spending time with Jared, too?" Tabi wasn't sure if she was happy that Duncan wasn't jealous anymore, or if it bothered her that he was willing to share her with Jared.

"I'm not sure if all right is the best word for it. If I have my way you will eventually agree to become like me, and Jared can guard us both. A vampire's bloodlust and sexual appetites are powerful, and interlinked. In the beginning you will find it difficult to go very long without sex or feeding. Jared could help with both those needs, and I trust him to protect you as fiercely as he guards me."

Duncan's grip tightened. "You are going to be mine, Tabi. Make no mistake. But in some ways Jared also belongs to me, and I will not pretend that the idea of watching him with you is repugnant. I would enjoy witnessing your pleasure with him." His hand moved higher. "And if you are willing, I would like very much for both of us to do all we can to please you. Together."

A flood of erotic images surged through Tabi's brain, making it hard to remember to breathe. "You really want the three of us to be together?" She finally managed to string together the words to a complete sentence.

"Yes, I do." Duncan's voice was a low rumble, and when she glanced over at him she could see the glow in his eyes had grown brighter.

"Have you and Jared..." She trailed off, not sure how to ask what was on her mind.

"Jared and I need to exchange a small amount of blood occasionally. It allows him to be linked to me, and gives him a small portion of my gifts. Speed, dexterity, strength, and of course, he doesn't age. We've never had a sexual relationship. I love him like a brother, not a lover."

"And the blood exchange?"

"Crystal goblet for me, shooter glass for him."

Duncan grinned broadly and she caught a glimpse of his fangs again. "He doesn't like the taste."

Tabi burst out laughing. "No, I bet he doesn't. I should probably confess I'm sort of squeamish about blood myself."

"I know." Duncan winked at her. "You try to hide it, but I've seen the way you go a little green around the gills when you see blood, which makes your decision to work in medicine a bit of an odd choice."

"My high school guidance counselor suggested it to me. I took the course because I knew I would be able to use the skills anywhere, and I was already planning on getting out of New York. It was a good fit, and it pays well enough."

Duncan gave her an odd look. "Do you like it? It doesn't sound like you do."

Tabi mulled that over. No one had ever asked her if she liked what she did. It was just what she had to do to stay alive and free from her family. "I don't dislike it. It's just work."

"Then quit."

"Quit? And do what? Starve? Go stark raving bananas from boredom? I can't just quit!"

"Of course you can." Duncan glanced over at her again, still grinning. "You're still not getting what I'm offering, lover. Stay and help me spend my money. Live with us and let us take care of you. You're not in this world alone anymore. Not if you don't want to be."

His words struck a chord deep in Tabi's soul. Duncan was offering her everything she'd ever dreamed of. All she had to do was trust him. That was the problem. Trusting people wasn't something she knew how to do.

Instead of speaking, she placed her hand over his as she fought back the emotions that threatened to overwhelm her. Tabi wanted more than anything to say yes, but there were too many doubts, too many uncertainties. And let's not forget he's a damned vampire, or the fact he's offering you a three-way relationship with another immortal hunk, she reminded herself sharply.

Duncan turned his hand over and threaded his fingers through hers. "You don't have to answer me now. I just wanted you to understand what's already yours when you're ready to accept it. I know this is something you need to think about. You see, three hundred and forty some odd years ago, a vampire made me the same offer. And when he did, I wasn't able to say yes to it either. Not right away."

"And he waited for you?"

"Yes, he did. And we stayed together for more than a century."

"So where is he now? Why aren't you together anymore?"

Duncan laughed. "He fell in love and I left them to enjoy their lives together."

"So you weren't with them the way you and Jared want to be with me?"

"Gods no. Natasha is like my little sister. I never thought of her that way. She and Gabriel live in London these days. When you're ready, we'll go meet them."

"Back up a step. Did you just suggest I meet your vampire family?"

"I did." Duncan gave her a look that oozed challenge. "Is there a problem with that?"

"Not so long as you don't expect that to happen any time soon."

"I told you, nothing happens until you're ready. I'm immortal, lover. I can wait as long as you need me to."

"And assuming I do agree to this, you have to promise that you will never ask to meet my family."

Duncan snarled something under his breath and she saw his eyes flare gold for a split second.

"Duncan? Is something wrong?"

"Nay. Just know that if I ever meet your family, they'll not be surviving the encounter. Not after all they've put you through."

"You know, I could get used to having you and Jared sticking up for me all the time." Tabi felt her fears lose a little more ground as she finally understood what it meant to know that someone was watching out for her. She'd never had that growing up, and the foreign sensation was a balm to her battered heart.

"You're part of our life now, Tabi. That won't change. I've told you the truth about our existence, and that means I'm responsible for you. You're under my sworn protection from now until the day you die. That will never change."

A sense of dread seeped into Tabi's mind. You mean the way you were responsible for Ruth?"

Duncan snarled again. "No. Not like Ruth. Ruth was a coldhearted bitch who lied and manipulated me at every turn. I found her on the street, fighting for her life against a gang of men intent on rape and mayhem. I saved her out of mercy, but when I went to wipe her mind she had the will to resist to me and I knew I had found one of the rare humans who could not be influenced by my kind. All guardians share that talent. Else what good would they be if they could be ordered to step aside for the first vampire who commanded them to do so? She was fierce and brave, and I was very taken with her."

"You loved her," Tabi said, and she felt a pang of unreasonable jealousy for a woman who had been gone from Duncan's life before Tabi had even been born.

"I did. At least I thought I did. The years have made me question if I ever truly loved her, or if I simply craved companionship and acceptance like my sire had found. Ruth gave me everything I wanted, but in the end, it was all a lie. The moment I gave her the power she craved, she turned on me and then fled to wreak destruction and bloodshed on an unsuspecting world. You are nothing like her, and what I feel for you is very different than what I felt for her." His hand closed around hers in a fierce grip. "I had to hunt her down because she was a risk to vampires everywhere. She killed for the fun of it, flaunting what she was to the world. I killed her for her betrayals, and hunting her down nearly destroyed me."

"But you didn't kill her." Tabi knew she was treading dangerous ground here, but she had to know.

"I thought I had. I left her staked to the ground of her den, her heart pierced. I brought down the roof of the cavern on top of her. She should have been dead and sealed in forever. I never thought..."

Tabi waited in silence for him to finish, but Duncan

didn't say another word until they pulled into the driveway of his home. *Their* home.

When he finally spoke, his voice was thick with regret. "It never occurred to me that she'd create another vampire. Ruth was still a fledgling, she shouldn't have had the strength to do that, not without help. She must have though. She created her own fledgling, and he found her and restored her somehow. You were hurt last night because I misjudged her. I will always regret that."

"If I hadn't been hurt, you would never have told me any of this. We would never have had this chance. I don't regret anything that's happened." Tabi meant every word, and as her new home came into view she accepted that this was where she was meant to be. She wasn't ready to agree with everything Jared and Duncan hoped to have from her, but she had taken her first steps down that path.

CHAPTER 8

TABI WOKE up with a beam of sunlight warming her face and a strong arm draped over her waist. Her first thought was that it was Duncan, but as her sleep-addled brain started working again she remembered him kissing her good night and tucking her into bed just a few hours before dawn. If Duncan was asleep in his quarters that meant that she was currently sharing her bed with—

"Good morning, mouse." Jared's soft drawl interrupted her musings. "Sleep well?"

"I did. So well I didn't notice when you snuck into bed with me. Is it really still morning?"

"Just barely. It's almost noon. Duncan said you went to bed around four, so I thought it was time you were up and around." Jared nuzzled at her hair, his breath warming the back of her neck.

"Is this how you wake up all your houseguests?" Tabi teased.

"You're not a guest anymore. Duncan told me you've agreed to live here," Jared pointed out, his large hand moving up her body to cup a breast through the cotton T-shirt she'd opted to wear to bed. She wasn't sure which one of them it belonged to, and she didn't care. She just liked wearing their things.

"For the record, you're the only woman I've woken up this way since I joined up with Duncan, guest or otherwise. I'm hoping you're going to be the only one I wake up this way for a long time to come, too."

"No one else? How's that possible? You're gorgeous! Surely there've been women in your life?"

"Not many, and not for very long. Can you see me dating? I'd have to lie, and that's no way to start a relationship. Not to mention that guarding Duncan is more than just my job, it's a lifetime commitment. It was easier to stay single and avoid the heartache."

Tabi snuggled herself tightly against Jared's side and turned her head to give him a sleepy smile as she observed, "You've both been lonely."

"We were. But we're not going to be anymore, because we found you." His thumb teased over her nipple as he placed a slow, tender trail of open-mouthed kisses down Tabi's neck.

She felt her pussy react with an instant flood of moisture, but she forced herself to stay in control, at least for now. There was something she needed to say first. "I slept with Duncan last night," she blurted out and then winced, wishing she could call a do-over.

"I know. He told me. He said you were incredible, and he regrets every second he spent talking himself out of being with you." Jared rubbed his rock-hard cock against the curve of her hip as he made it clear that Duncan's news hadn't affected his interest at all. "I'd like to find out for myself." Jared's breath caressed her cheek as he leaned over her. "Let me make love to you, Tabi."

"Yes please," she whispered, reaching back to touch him at last and discovering nothing but naked, muscular flesh beneath her hand.

Jared's rich laugh filled her ear as he toyed with her breast. "I was very optimistic you'd be agreeable, so I took the liberty of getting naked before joining you in bed."

Tabi laughed as she stroked his bare thigh. "And if I'd said no?"

"Then I'd have done my damnedest to convince you to change your mind. I can be a very determined man when I need to be." His hand moved away from her breast just long enough to slide beneath her shirt before returning to its former place. "I couldn't think of anything but you last night. You haunted my dreams."

Jared's head loomed over hers and brushed a slow, lingering kiss to her lips. "When Duncan told me you were staying, it was all I could do to let you sleep."

Tabi rolled onto her side to face him, her hands stealing up to span the massive expanse of Jared's chest. Her fingers stroked through the smattering of red-gold hairs she found there before she teased her way down to his nipples, which hardened the instant she touched them.

"You're sure?" she asked, but his answer was already evident as he nearly tore the T-shirt from her body in his eagerness to get it off her.

The moment he succeeded in stripping it over her head he hauled her up against him. "I've never been so damned sure of anything in all my life," he vowed as he folded her into his arms. "You're ours, honey. Never doubt it." His lips met hers and fire washed over her skin. Jared's big hands were everywhere, hungrily exploring every inch of her body he could reach as he kissed her so deeply her lungs burned and her blood sang with need.

Jared was big all over, from his broad chest to the thick, clever fingers he was using to rocket her straight into the stratosphere. Reaching between them Tabi gasped as she confirmed that his cock was as large as the rest of him, so thick she could barely span it with her fingers. Her touch had him groaning and his hips jerked forward, sliding her hand up the hard length of his shaft.

"Goddamn that feels good!"

Tabi gripped him a little harder, sliding her hand from the base up to the tip of his cock. She found the head already slick with pre-cum and she spread it back down his cock with her next stroke, earning another low groan. Jared's kisses grew harder as she worked his dick with her hands and he reached down to part her thighs, growling with approval as he found her folds already slick and wet with need.

"I want to see if your pussy is as pretty as the rest of you," he rasped as he ran a finger around her clit. "Show me."

He tore the covers off of them both and moved away from her enough he could see every part of her. Tabi let him look his fill, the lust in his eyes reassuring her that she didn't have to hide or be embarrassed by her body.

She released his cock and reached her arms over her head and arched her back in a catlike stretch, her eyes never leaving his handsome face as she basked in the molten heat of his gaze. She had spent most of her life feeling self-conscious about her height and lack of curves, but when Jared or Duncan looked at her, all she felt was beautiful.

Jared's hands landed on her thighs and he parted them wider, settling himself on his knees in the newly formed space between her legs.

"Don't you go telling him I said so, but Duncan's an idiot. He should have taken one look at you and done whatever it took to get you here and naked, I know I would have."

"I'm here now." Tabi lifted her hands toward Jared. "And even though I'm probably insane to even consider taking up with two men, I want you. So stop talking and show me why I'm not making the biggest mistake of my life."

"Brave talk for a mouse." Jared grinned and slid his hands under her ass, lifting her lower half off the bed as though she weighed next to nothing at all. Before she could determine what he was up to Tabi found herself half suspended with her legs draped over Jared's shoulders and only her head and shoulders touching the bed.

"What are you—" was all she managed to say before he buried his face into her cunt and began to devour her. His tongue flicked over her clit in short, lightning fast swipes that had her seeing stars as his hands kneaded her ass cheeks. Helpless to do anything but dangle from his hands, Tabi gasped and fisted her hands in the bed sheets, completely overwhelmed by the delicious sensations unfurling from her pussy. "So...oh gods so good!" She shuddered as the first tremors of an orgasm rippled outward and then mewled in protest as his mouth slowed, denying her the release she craved.

Jared controlled the pace, sweeping his tongue along her inner folds in long, languid strokes that felt incredible but left her swollen clit untouched. Sensations layered themselves on her awareness, but above them all was the pulsing ache of her clitoris. Jared worked her body like a maestro, feasting on her pussy until Tabi hung on the edge of an orgasm, suspended and trembling until Jared gave her what she needed. She knew a single touch of his mouth to her clit would set her off, but Jared denied her and sexual frustration finally broke through Tabi's control.

"Let me come! Please?" She was begging now and felt the vibrations of Jared's satisfied chuckle reverberate through her. Instead of giving in, Jared slid a finger deep into her slick cunt and then removed it again before Tabi could use it to help push herself over the edge. Again he chuckled, and Tabi snarled in frustration and wriggled her hips, trying to get his mouth where she needed it the most. Again his thick finger pressed inside her and was gone, a teasing echo of what she really needed right now. She needed his cock inside her, fucking her until they were both too tired to move.

Tabi groaned and then her breath caught in her throat as she felt his fingertip press against the rosebud of her anus, stroking tiny circles around it.

Without a word of warning he pressed deeper,

working past the ring of tight muscles. She knew enough to relax and not tighten up around him, easy enough to do when his mouth was doing incredible things to her pussy to help distract her. His head moved and Jared's tongue stabbed into her cunt, fucking her like a small cock as he worked his finger the rest of the way in. The double stimulation was more than Tabi's body could take and she came hard, grinding herself against Jared's mouth as his hand did wicked things to her ass, making her come even harder.

When Tabi finally managed to open her eyes she was greeted by Jared's handsome face smiling smugly as he tenderly eased her shaking legs from his shoulders and lowered her back to the bed. Tremors and aftershocks still made it hard to think clearly and her limbs felt too heavy, but she reached for Jared anyway, needing him close.

"You are even more beautiful when you're coming," he told her as he took her hand and pressed a kiss to the tip of each finger. "I'm going to make it my mission in life to make you look like that as often as I can."

Tabi laughed and groaned at the same time. "Between the two of you I may never need to go to a gym again."

"Wait until we take you on at the same time." Jared's grin turned sinful. "I bet you sleep for a week afterward."

"The two of you together..." Tabi's mind reeled as she let her imagination run away with her for a minute, thinking of what it might be like to share her body and her bed with both her lovers at the same time. "It might kill me, but it would be worth it."

"I can think of worse ways to go," Jared agreed as his

hands wandered over her body, teasing and touching as they drifted gently here and there. "Reality moment here, do I need to go grab some condoms? Or are you protected?"

"I get the shot," she told him and then tensed. "But Duncan and I...should we have?"

"Neither he nor I are susceptible to disease or infection. You're completely safe. Vampires can't have children either, so I'm the only one we need to be worried about knocking you up."

"Good to know." Tabi curled her hand around his nearly erect cock and stroked it from root to head, pleased to note the low groan of pleasure even her slight touch drew from Jared.

"Do that again, mouse, and I'm going to show you what happens when you tease a man with a hard-on."

Tabi laughed and accepted the challenge by repeating her action, only her grip was firmer this time.

Before she could so much as blink she found herself sprawled across Jared's chest, his hands on her hips and his powerful frame stretched out underneath hers. The hard shaft of his dick was pinned along the length of her pussy, already coated in the slick evidence of her earlier orgasm.

Jared helped her keep her balance as she drew herself up onto her knees and ground her pussy against his cock, making both of them moan.

"That's right, just like that." Jared's voice was thick with lust and his eyes were gleaming with a green-gray light that reminded Tabi of the supernatural glow of Duncan's eyes.

"Your eyes are glowing," she whispered and Jared grinned. "Well that's never happened before. That's your doing, mouse." He bumped his hips upward, encouraging her to move again.

"I need to be inside you. Need to feel you fucking me. Now."

"I need you, too," Tabi whispered and was stunned to realize just how much she meant it. She'd been with Duncan last night, and it had been amazing, but this was Jared, and he was as special to her in his way as Duncan was.

Holy shit, I'm falling in love with both of them.

She was still reeling from that revelation as she rose up on her knees and reached between them to line up Jared's cock, settling her body around the wide head of his dick with a shocked moan as he stretched her entrance wide. Once he was in far enough she let gravity take over and she moved her hand from between them to clamp around his wrist, holding herself steady as she took him inch by inch into her body.

He was big enough that she felt her body giving way and stretching to accommodate him until he was so deep inside her she felt impossibly, incredibly full. She gave an experimental pulse of her inner muscles and Jared's fingers tightened into her hips. "Fuck, yes. Do that again!"

She clamped his cock tighter this time and he grunted with pleasure. "You were tight before, but when you do that? Holy fuck."

"Kegel exercises, a girl's best friend." Tabi grinned as she leaned forward and kissed him, rolling her hips in a slow figure-eight pattern as her mouth brushed over his.

"You're killing me," Jared groaned and pushed his hips up off the bed, lifting her with him and stealing the breath from her lungs as his cock filled her completely.

"Nuh-uh." Tabi shook her head to clear away the stars flashing in the corners of her vision and pinched his nipple sharply. "It's my turn, you lie still."

"Lie still? Are you kidding me?!" He lowered them both back to the bed and grumbled, "Meek, my ass!"

"You teased me and now I get to tease you," she purred back at him and started her slow, sinuous movements again. Every twist sent shimmers of pleasure sparkling through her body and her breasts rubbed over his chest, adding a delicious friction that had her nipples hard and hypersensitive to the slightest contact. Jared's hands left her hips and he worked his fingers between their bodies to toy with the tightened nubs and it was all Tabi could do to keep to her plan to build their love-making up slowly. That's what this was, lovemaking. She'd been fucked before, but this was something else, a forging of a bond that she knew was going to alter her life forever. She'd spent her whole adult life looking for this kind of connection and never found it. And now she'd found it twice in twenty-four hours with two different men. She kissed Jared intently, her tongue twining with his as she took him deep and then eased their bodies apart until they were barely touching, only to start the dance over again with her next movement. Even she was starting to believe in fate now. It was hard *not* to believe after everything that had happened in the past two days.

Time stretched out and the world faded into the background to leave the two of them entangled in each other's pleasure, and away from every other distraction. Tabi started moving faster and her control began to crack as the demands of her body to break free and fly grew stronger with every passing second. Jared bucked beneath her and she rode him like a galloping stallion, her hands gripping the pillow beside his head as their bodies came together and parted again in a breakneck rhythm that had them both racing toward the oblivion of release.

Jared's hands caught at her hips as he lifted her up a few inches, giving him the clearance he needed to drive himself into her pussy at will. Hard and fast he pounded into her, the breath sawing in and out of his lungs between hungry kisses and wild cries of her name.

Tabi was teetering on the edge and sat up, one hand clamping around Jared's forearm as the fingers of her free hand slipped into her pussy to touch her clit.

Jared's gray-green eyes flashed with heat as he lifted his head to watch her play with herself just at the point their bodies joined and a feral grin curved over his lips. "Holy Fuck! That's beautiful!" he groaned and Tabi felt Jared's body go rigid beneath hers as an orgasm tore through him. The muscles on his chest and stomach stood out in relief as his body bucked upward hard enough to lift Tabi from the bed. Her fingers were pushed hard against her tender clitoris and Tabi's world exploded into fragments of light and sound that danced around the room.

Her release was so intense she forgot to breathe, and when her senses returned she sucked in a lungful of air like a freestyle diver breaking the ocean's surface after a long dive. Jared's big body settled back onto the bed and she slumped against his chest with her heart pounding and her limbs trembling. Jared's arms came around her, cradling her against him as he turned his head and brushed a breathless kiss to the corner of her mouth.

"In case I haven't made it clear already, I am damned glad you've decided to stay here with us. It saves me having to get down on my knees and beg, because after that there is no way in hell I am ever letting you go."

Tabi laughed and a ribbon of something that felt like pure sunshine wrapped itself around her heart. "I'm not going anywhere. All my life I've been dreaming of having a knight ride in and rescue me from my family. Now that I've made my own escape, I find two of them. Why on earth would I leave?"

"If you call Duncan a knight in shining armor I think he loses a vampire merit badge," Jared snickered. "You're one brave woman you know, taking us both on."

"What's to be brave about?" she quipped and looked into Jared's eyes. "Apart from those minor issues of Duncan being a vampire, you being his mostly immortal minion and oh yes, the fact that Duncan's fanged, psychotic ex is out there planning her revenge, I'd say things are coming up sunshine and roses."

Jared cupped her cheek in one massive palm and stared up into her eyes. "We won't let anything happen to you, Tabi. I swear it."

"It's not me I'm worried about. You two need to take care of each other. I don't think I'm the one she's looking to kill."

His sigh filled the room. "No, I don't think you're her target either. She's going to go after Duncan."

Tabi laid her head on Jared's chest so that the thump-thump of his heartbeat sounded in her ear. "Then we'll have to keep *him* safe. I just found you two and I'm not losing either of you."

CHAPTER 9

WHEN THEY'D FINALLY GOTTEN out of bed Tabi had indulged herself in another long, hot soak in the pool-sized bathtub while Jared had fixed them both something to eat. As they'd shared a meal he'd finally told her the rest of the story of how he met Duncan, and his story had made Tabi's heart ache for the man he'd been so many years ago.

Born soon after the turn of the century to a family of ranchers, Jared lost the land he had inherited from his parents during the Great Depression. His fiancée had broken off their engagement to marry a wealthy man and Jared had set out for the west hoping for employment. Instead he had witnessed the brutal carnage left behind by Ruth when she had attacked a transient camp the night before he'd arrived there. He had still been digging graves for the dead when Duncan had found him the following evening. Jared had felt certain that destiny had put the two men together, and by dawn he had been in

Duncan's service. Half-starved, destitute and alone, Tabi had no doubt that Duncan's offer must have seemed like divine intervention.

It was hard for her to look at Jared and know that he had been in his prime when the Great Depression had rocked the country. Not when he looked to be only a little older than her twenty-four years. Somehow it was easier to accept Duncan's far greater age than it was to know that Jared was the same generation as her great-grand-parents.

"Penny for your thoughts?" Jared interrupted her musings with a grin.

Tabi grinned. "I was just thinking that the two of you must really have a thing for younger women."

For a second Jared was speechless and then he threw back his head and guffawed until tears rolled down his cheeks.

"I'm going to tell Duncan you said that, and he's going to have words for you!"

"What, he's going to turn his little girl over his knee?" The words were out of her mouth before Tabi had a chance to run them through her self-edit mode and she blushed as Jared burst into another round of laughter.

"I'm sure he'd be more than happy to do it if I asked him nicely. I'd forgo coffee for a week just to see your pretty little ass spanked until it was pink."

"You wouldn't!" Tabi gawked and spluttered even while dark arousal pooled in the back of her mind and made her squirm slightly in her seat.

"Hell yes I would." Jared's eyes gleamed with lust at

the thought. "And then afterward I could kiss it all better."

"Dream on, McDuff. That is never, ever going to happen." Tabi pushed back from the table and gathered up the remains of their meal, buying herself a few seconds to get her wayward libido back under control before Jared noticed her body's response didn't match the words coming out of her mouth.

"Methinks the lady doth protest too much."

Shit. He noticed. A well-muscled arm wrapped around her and tugged her up against Jared's chest as his lips nuzzled that spot just below her ear. Tabi's heart did a triple beat in her chest and she felt her knees give way as he dropped several butterfly-soft kisses to the same spot.

"You like the idea, don't you?" His voice caressed her skin like warm silk.

"No." Tabi tried to get her legs to hold her weight but they rebelled.

"Liar." Jared nipped at her throat and she felt the contact zing from her neck straight to her pussy, which began to grow damp. "Come on, 'fess up. You liked the idea of being spanked. You like the idea of the two of us teasing and touching you at the same time." He kissed away the sting and blew a puff of air across her skin. "I know I like it, a hell of a lot. I can't wait until you're ready to do that with us. So admit it, mouse. You want it. You want to find out what it would be like." Jared's voice dropped to a husky rumble. "It's going to be incredible. I'm going to take that pretty ass while you're fucking

Duncan, and the two of us are going to make you forget any other man you've ever been with."

"You are?" Tabi's mind reeled at the images Jared was planting in her head and she could feel her panties had gone from damp to drenched at the erotic, wicked thoughts racing through her brain.

"Mmhmm. And you are going to love every minute of it, I promise."

Tabi turned her head so she could see Jared's face. "Last night, Duncan didn't feed from me because he knew I wasn't ready. I'm afraid it's going to hurt," she confessed it all quickly, embarrassed to admit to fear.

"It won't hurt."

"But when that other vampire bit me..." She trailed off and touched her neck. "That really hurt!"

"His attack on you was deliberately savage, sending a message to Duncan. It doesn't have to be like that, he did it on purpose. I've only been bitten once. That first time we did a blood transfer, Duncan bit me. I came right then and there, without so much as a caress. It was the most incredible orgasm I have ever experienced." Jared laughed and hugged her. "That is, until today."

"You did? But I thought you two weren't involved, uh, that way."

"We're not. He couldn't explain it very well at the time, but years of study and medical research gave him the answer. Vampires can choose to excrete an enzyme in their saliva that acts as an aphrodisiac. An extremely powerful one that starts working the moment it hits the bloodstream. It gives other vampires a nice buzz and ramps up their sex drive, and on us humans it works even better."

"Why didn't he tell me that?"

"Probably because he didn't want to feel that he'd bribed you into letting him feed from you before you were ready just because of what you might experience. He wants you to come to him willingly, Tabi. Every step of the way. He's got a rule that he never breaks. He will never feed from anyone without permission. Not ever."

"That's a good rule," Tabi murmured, her mind busy as she sorted through all this new information.

"He used to have another one. He swore he'd never change another human into a vampire. Not after Ruth. You changed that, mouse. Changed him. I think you should consider it. There's a lot to be said for the life he's offering you."

"If it's such a good life, why haven't you asked to become like him? Surely he'd break his rule for you after all this time?"

"Two reasons. First, because I knew he wasn't ready, and the second, most important reason is this: if I became like him, who would be left to watch over him when he was vulnerable? He needs me."

AFTER LUNCH JARED had given Tabi a proper tour of the house, showing her all the amenities to her new home. The indoor pool had delighted her and when he'd taken her down to the garage to see Duncan's collection of vehicles she had laughed so hard she'd had to lean up against the wall until she caught her breath. There was no doubt in Jared's mind that Duncan would be hearing Tabi's opinion on the dozen or so luxury sports cars and motorcycles he currently owned. If she could manage to spit the words out between gales of laughter, that is.

There was another reason for the guided tour. Tabi needed to be familiar with the extensive security measures the protected the entire property. He pointed out the heat-and-motion-activated cameras and showed her where the subtly hidden panic alarms were located. From anywhere in the house, she was never more than a few steps away from help. Duncan may be the obvious target, but Jared had no intention of leaving anything to chance.

Only once he was sure Tabi was secure and settled did he head out on errands. Along with his usual groceries, he'd gotten a list of Tabi's favorite foods and they'd done a bit of menu planning for the week. Jared was looking forward to having someone *else* cook for a change, that was for damn sure. He also had another shopping list that had nothing to do with food, a list that he and Duncan had put together while Tabi slept upstairs. He let loose with a wicked chuckle as he imagined her reaction to the selection of toys he was planning on bringing back for them to play with. Not even Ruth's thirst for vengeance was going to put a damper on their celebration of Tabi's decision to stay with them.

He grabbed the keys to the Porsche 911 coupe that had set off Tabi's giggles earlier that day. She may not understand the attraction of the candy-apple-black custom paint job and the vehicle's elegant lines, but he certainly did. With an affectionate pat on the steering wheel Jared started the car and headed out. He had a lot to do in the few hours of daylight he had left.

Two hours later he was racing the sunset, the back-seat loaded with groceries and several discreetly wrapped packages he planned on smuggling into the house later while Tabi was distracted. She didn't know it yet, but he and Duncan had plans for her tonight. Just thinking about it made him hard, and he had to shift in his seat as his dick pressed uncomfortably tight against the fly of his jeans. "Hands on the wheel and eyes on the road or you're going to end up in the ditch instead of in bed with Tabi tonight," he muttered to himself as he made the final turn onto their street and headed for the gates of home. Tonight couldn't get here fast enough.

He walked into the kitchen and immediately knew something wasn't right. Dinner had been partially prepared, but nothing was cooking and the room was empty. Jared set the bags down on the counter and went to the nearest security panel to check on things. The double row of green lights reassured him, and he headed deeper into the house, looking for his charges.

"Hello? Where'd you guys go?" he called down the hall and he was further relieved when Duncan answered.

"Jared? Glad you're home. You're going to want to see this. We're in the entertainment room." Duncan's tone was strained, and Jared knew right off that their plans for the evening were about to change for the worse. When he walked into the room and saw Tabi's tearstained face it was all the confirmation he needed.

"What happened?" he asked, already making a

beeline for Tabi. Duncan released her from his arms and she fell into Jared's with a relieved sigh.

"I was worried something had happened to you, it's getting dark out." She exclaimed and hugged him. "And you weren't answering your phone earlier."

"I had it on vibrate and forgot about it. I'm sorry, mouse. I didn't mean to worry you. But what has you upset? I know I'm the center of your world now, but I wasn't gone long enough for you to even miss me!"

Tabi chuckled softly and hugged him tighter. "The center of my world, huh? Did you hit your head while you were out?"

Pleased to see her smiling again, Jared wrapped her in his arms and looked over her head at Duncan. "What happened?"

"A vampire went on a killing spree last night." Duncan's eyes were shadowed with regret as he met Jared's gaze. "The kills are too neat for it to have been Ruth, so it must have been her minion, the one that attacked Tabi the other night. Only this time he didn't settle for a single messenger. According to the news reports there were half a dozen deaths between midnight and sunrise." He pointed to the muted television that took up most of one wall of the room. It was currently showing a well-coiffed anchorman talking to the camera. Photographs of different crime scenes and sobbing relatives flashed up and were then replaced with other images, just as terrible. "The victims were taken from all over the city, but their bodies were placed very carefully. There was one found on each of the streets that mark the borders of my territory. The message is clear. They're going to turn my home into a killing field until I stop them."

Duncan's mouth was pressed into a grim line and he suddenly looked every inch a predator as he rose to his full height and clenched his hand into a fist. "I've been waiting for you to come home so we can discuss tactics. She needs to be stopped."

Jared nodded, already knowing there could be no other way for this to play out. "You're going after her." It wasn't a question.

"I have to. But that leaves one key question." Duncan arched a brow at Jared in silent query and then dropped his gaze to Tabi.

"You can't go out there alone, Duncan. She'll be safer here than anywhere else in the city."

Tabi lifted her head and then twisted herself around in Jared's arms so she could see them both. "Of course I'll be safe here. You need Jared to watch your back, Duncan. This was all done on purpose to challenge you and draw you out of the one place they can't breach. Somewhere out there Ruth and her pet psychopath are waiting for you. I'll be fine here."

Jared had a brainwave and interrupted Duncan before he could disagree. "We'll tuck Tabi into bed in your quarters, Duncan. That's the most secure place in the entire house. Nothing short of a demolition team or an act of god is getting past those doors."

Duncan nodded once. "Good thinking."

"So you're locking me in Duncan's bunker for the night?" Tabi didn't look as pleased with his idea as Jared had expected. "I'm not a puppy you can kennel or some delicate flower of womanhood that will faint at the first broken nail!"

Duncan covered the space between them in a heartbeat and Jared just held onto Tabi as Duncan leaned down and flashed his fangs, his eyes gleaming an intense shade of amber. "It's not the fact you're a woman that has me worried. It's the fact you're human. You can't protect yourself from one of my kind. Ruth and *her pet psycho* as you put it are out there killing innocents right now, and I can't stop it until I know you are safe. You need to be somewhere that she can't find you, because the only thing in the world that would stop me from killing her is if she used you as a shield or a bartering chip. You're too important to me, Tabi. You're the chink in my armor."

"Mine too," Jared added. "I won't be able to concentrate if I don't know for certain you're safe and sound. Will you please do this for us?"

"You guys don't play fair," Tabi grumbled and swept a lock of Duncan's hair back from his face, apparently completely unfazed by his fangs and glowing eyes. "Neither of you." She glanced back to give Jared a crooked smile that made his heart melt a little around the edges.

"So is that a yes?" Jared asked as he smiled back at her, grateful she had stopped arguing with them.

"That's a yes. So stop doing the glowy-eyed cranky vampire thing already, Duncan. I'll bunk down in your quarters." She frowned. "At least I will once you promise me there isn't a creepy coffin down there anywhere."

Jared snickered and Duncan growled in disdain. "I don't sleep in a coffin, thank you. I have a very nice suite, with a king-sized bed you're more than welcome to share with me anytime you like."

"Yeah, along with a computer, big screen TV, digital cable, and about a thousand movies on Blu-ray and surround sound. You'll never want to leave."

Tabi laughed and kissed Duncan before turning and brushing her sweet mouth over Jared's too. "A vampire with a man-cave and a garage full of testosterone-soaked toys." She paused and then smirked at Jared. "And a butler. I think Jared had it wrong. You're not the Highlander. You're Batman."

"Oh god, not you too," Duncan groaned and shook his head. "What did I do to deserve two smart-mouthed companions? Tabi, go find whatever you're going to want to take downstairs. Once you're there you're not coming out again until morning."

"I'll whip us up something fast to eat while you get sorted, mouse. See you back here in ten minutes." That would be enough time for Duncan and him to begin making their plans for the night. Once they had Tabi secured, they'd be going hunting, and Jared knew from experience that it was going to be a very long night. Hunting for someone who knew you were looking for them wasn't just difficult, it was damned dangerous.

As Tabi's footsteps receded up the stairway, he and Duncan headed for the kitchen. Jared couldn't help but feel guilty that while he and Tabi had been enjoying their time together, they'd missed the news about the murders. He should have been keeping an eye on things better than that. He should have been expecting Ruth to make a move, but he'd been distracted by Tabi. Duncan was right, she was the chink in both their armor. He couldn't afford to be distracted again. This time it meant they'd lost hours of preparation and planning time. If he let it happen again, he could lose a whole lot more. That wasn't going to happen. Jared vowed that he'd die before he let anything happen to either of them. After all, that was his job, and the two of them were the most important people in his life.

Once they got Tabi settled and secured downstairs, they set to work preparing for the night's work. They met in the hall between their bedrooms, both of them dressed in dark clothing and heavy leather jackets that would provide them at least some protection from blades and claws and fangs. They were both armed with stakes, swords and wicked-looking knives, and Jared couldn't help but reflect that they were a grim looking pair as they headed down the curved staircase. Their battle gear clashed with the polished wood paneling and old-fashioned banister, and part of him was grateful that Tabi wouldn't see them like this. Once she'd had time to get used to the darker elements of their world then this wouldn't be such a shock, but for now Jared just wanted to keep her safe and ease her into the life he and Duncan wanted for her. A life with them.

Jared waited until they were in the SUV to broach the topic he'd been mulling over since the moment he'd gotten home and found out what he'd missed. "I'm sorry I missed the news about the murders. I should have been on top of that, and I wasn't."

Duncan was silent for a moment and then lifted a hand from the steering wheel in a dismissive gesture.

"What's done is done. I'm not sure that knowing about it any sooner would have helped us concoct a better plan, and you are entitled to have a life outside your duties to me." Duncan's eyes were glowing slightly as he looked over at Jared. "She's both of ours to protect, and to cherish. If you hadn't taken the time to show her around the house today and teach her how the security works, we couldn't have both gone out tonight. Now we both know she's safe, and we can focus on what needs to be done."

Jared's adrenaline levels started to climb as they headed into the city to start their hunt. "No sweat, boss. All we need to do is hunt down a rogue vampire or two in a city of more than two and a half million people while avoiding getting hunted ourselves. Not to mention we have to do it without upsetting the nice, normal people. What could possibly go wrong with this plan?"

CHAPTER 10

"Tabi! Wake up and help me!" The demand pierced the warm, comforting veil of sleep and tore Tabi out of her dreams and into a waking nightmare. Jared flung on the lights and Tabi had to bite her tongue to clear away the nausea that immediately bubbled up inside her as she looked at the blood-soaked pair of hunters.

Duncan was barely able to stand, even with Jared's larger body supporting him. What she could see of his face was pale as death beneath the gory mask that covered most of his features. Even his blond hair hung in lank, bloody strings around his face.

"What the hell happened?" Tabi forced herself out of bed and to Duncan's side, slipping her arm around his waist as the two of them carried him over to the bed and settled him carefully onto the rumpled blankets.

Duncan wheezed with bitter laughter. "It didn't go quite the way I had intended."

"That's an understatement." Tabi started peeling off

Duncan's gore-splattered clothing, ignoring the churning of her stomach at the sight of all the blood. The dove-gray duvet beneath Duncan's body was already stained crimson with it, and there seemed to be more every second. Still, this was Duncan and she was just going to have to get over her hang up, because there was no way she was going to run off and be sick. Not when he needed her.

Claw marks had torn through his clothes at several points, and when she finally got his shirt off she found a vicious slice that ran diagonally across his chest from shoulder to flank. "Holy shit, what did this?"

"A sword," Duncan hissed, his eyes closed against the pain. "A very fucking sharp one."

"I didn't know they came any other way," Tabi muttered and used part of his shirt to wipe away more of the blood. "This will heal quickly, won't it? I know you heal super fast, so I'm hoping this isn't as bad as it looks."

Duncan grabbed Tabi's hand and squeezed it tightly. "I'll be all right. It'll just take a while, a few days at least."

Jared rumbled angrily from the bottom of the bed where he'd been busy stripping off Duncan's ruined pants and boots. "Don't be an ass, boss. You know we don't have a few days. You need to feed."

Tabi's head snapped up. "Then go get him what he needs. Surely he keeps a supply down here?"

Duncan nodded but Jared growled again. "What he doesn't want me to tell you is that he'll heal faster from fresh blood, and I'm banged up enough I need all I have to heal myself…"

"Oh." Understanding dawned and Tabi didn't hesitate. "Then he better feed from me."

"No," Duncan growled his denial and his eyes opened again to glare up at Tabi and then at Jared. "I told you not to tell her because I don't want her to feel pressured to do something she's not ready for!"

"Martyrdom doesn't suit you, sexy. Drop it," Tabi snapped, her decision already made. "You need to feed, and I'm the only one here who wasn't just the recipient of a serious beat down, so stop arguing and just do it. Jared's right, you don't have days to recover."

"You tell him, mouse." Jared chuckled and then stilled as she glowered at him.

"How badly hurt are *you*, Jared?"

"Battered and bruised, and a possible concussion but that's it. He waited for us to split up and then went after Duncan."

"I didn't detect his presence. Should have...doesn't make sense," Duncan muttered, his eyes closing again.

Tabi's insides were curdling with fear and anxiety at Duncan's weakened state. She had to help him. Jared seemed to share that opinion because he sat down on the edge of the bed and said, "We can talk about this later. Right now he needs to feed. Are you really up for this?"

"Would it matter if I weren't?" Tabi pointed out and then looked down at Duncan. "What do I do?"

"Just snuggle up beside him and make sure your throat is near his mouth. His instincts will take it from there. Don't worry, he's not so far gone that he'll hurt you." Jared grinned and Tabi caught something wicked dancing in the gray-green depths of his eyes. "In fact, I'm pretty sure you're going to enjoy it a helluva lot."

"Seriously? You're thinking about the side effects of his bite *now*?" Tabi couldn't believe Jared was thinking of sex at a time like this.

"I'm a guy, I'd have to be dead before I stop thinking about sex, especially when there's a half-naked goddess kneeling on a bed right in front of me."

Duncan's lips quirked into a slight grin and he murmured just loud enough to be heard. "She looks good in my bed, doesn't she?"

"You too? Are you both insane? This is first aid, not sexy time!" Tabi gave up arguing and settled down beside Duncan, pressing a kiss to his pale lips before turning so that her back was to his chest and her head rested by his shoulder. She moved her hair back and closed her eyes. "Take what you need, Duncan. I trust you."

"I'll never hurt you," he whispered as he moved in behind her and nuzzled the side of her neck, sending goose bumps chasing down her skin. "Need you so much," he murmured before feathering a kiss to her throat.

She braced herself for the pain, but as his fangs sank deep into her neck she felt nothing but a brief pinch and then a deep burn that set fire to her blood. Duncan groaned and drew her into his arms and she was amazed to feel his cock hardening against the small of her back. She was still wondering how that was possible when the effects of Duncan's bite kicked in and her entire body shuddered in the thrall of an orgasm so intense and sudden that she screamed. Tabi was caught up in a firestorm of pleasure so raw, hot, and intense she couldn't do anything but cling to Duncan and try to remember to breathe.

Jared's warm, spicy scent tickled her nose and she realized he had settled alongside her, his hands tearing away the shirt she'd worn to sleep in so that she was lying naked and safe between her two lovers.

"Is he making you feel good?" Jared asked and Tabi could only moan in response as another wave of bliss washed through her and swept away her ability to speak.

She felt hands stroke down her bare thigh, and then Jared's warm, naked body was pressed up against her as he lifted her leg back and over Duncan's thigh and reached down to stroke her sopping pussy.

"Oh he's got you so wet, honey. You don't know which way is up right now. Do you? I told you it was going to be incredible."

Jared's words sent Tabi crashing back over the brink again. Her pussy pulsed and tightened around empty space as Jared's fingers worked the delicate bundle of nerves hidden deep in her folds, making her babble breathlessly and then scream as he set off another series orgasmic waves.

Duncan's arms wrapped around her more firmly. He moved at last, lifting his head from her throat. "I need you," he groaned and pressed a kiss to the spot where he'd bitten her.

"She's yours." Jared's hand slipped out from between her legs and Tabi mewled in protest, only to lose her next breath to a needy gasp as Duncan positioned his cock and then thrust himself deep inside without changing their positions.

"Thank you," he whispered to Jared before coaxing Tabi to turn her head so he could slant his lips over hers in a scorching kiss that spoke volumes about his recovery status. The taste of her blood was on his lips and yet Tabi didn't care. She was still floating on a cloud of sexual bliss that left no room for any thought save her need for the two men in bed with her.

Jared shifted his position so he was sitting up, watching Duncan fuck her. Without thinking she reached out to Jared even as she kissed Duncan, her hand gliding over Jared's muscular thigh to wrap around his cock.

He groaned with approval and moved closer so she could stroke his entire length. "Goddamn, that's it. Yes, honey. Just like that. Fuck, that's so good. I could watch you get fucked forever."

Duncan chuckled faintly, the vibration rolling through his body to hers. "Does he always talk this much?"

"Yes. You'll get used to it," Tabi told him and both men growled.

"Did you just agree to us doing this on a regular basis?" Jared asked.

"I think I did," she answered, still too dreamy to worry about what she was agreeing to. She just knew what she wanted. She wanted both of them to touch her, to fuck her, to make love to her until the world went away. They were hers and she was never letting them go.

Duncan lifted up on one elbow to kiss her more easily

as his thrusts came deeper and faster. His mouth covered hers, muffling her cries of need. Soon she was lost in another sexual firestorm, her hand working Jared's cock as Duncan pumped into her, his strength and power demonstrating clearly that he was already nearly recovered.

"How?" she whispered between torrid kisses.

"You healed me, love."

Tabi opened her eyes and found herself lost in the blazing, golden glory of Duncan's gaze. He was looking down at her with an expression of such adoration that it felt as though he had bitten her again. Need sang through her veins and made her pussy clamp down hard on his cock as she tried to lock him into her body and her soul forever. Her free hand tunneled into the tangled locks of Duncan's hair and she wrapped it around her fingers before tugging his mouth down to hers. Ignoring his fangs, she parted her lips and invited his tongue to mate and twine with hers in a pantomime of the passionate dance their bodies shared.

Tabi only vaguely felt Jared's hand curl around hers to guide her strokes as she began ascending the stairs to heaven yet again. Duncan's every thrust drove them higher and higher, and she could hear the sensual groans of both men accompanying her own muffled cries. Her hand tightened around Jared's cock, taking him with them as she matched Duncan's pace with hips and fingers, racing both her men to ecstasy.

Just as she neared the peak, Duncan nipped her lower lip and sucked it into his mouth, sending another jolt of raw lust sizzling through her and knocking her off the edge and into the oblivion of an orgasm so strong she nearly drowned in it.

Somewhere in the distance she heard Duncan roar as he emptied himself inside her, and then jets of hot liquid coated her hand as Jared's voice joined Duncan's and he came as well. Tabi rode the waves of bliss for what seemed like an eternity, and she only vaguely sensed when her two lovers changed positions so that she was snuggled between them again.

When her wits finally returned and the effects of Duncan's bite eased a bit she heard the two of them talking in muffled tones.

"You could have warned me," she grumbled, her voice huskier than she expected, until it dawned on her it was because her throat was raw from all the screaming she'd been doing.

"I did warn you. So don't you go claiming otherwise." Jared's warm drawl buzzed near her ear and she turned her head to give him a soft, languid kiss.

"You said...but that was..." Tabi's hands fluttered weakly above her still mostly boneless body.

"Incredible." Duncan's voice rumbled in her other ear as his breath fanned over her cheek.

"Duncan?" Tabi tore her lips from Jared to turn over and look properly at Duncan. "Are you really okay?"

"Aye, lover. I'm fine. Another few minutes and I'll be as fit as if it never happened, which is more than I can say for the two of you." Duncan kissed her with such tender sweetness it took Tabi's breath away. "You shouldn't have fed me. You've barely regained what you lost in the attack the other night."

He glanced over Tabi to glower at Jared. "And you shouldn't have allowed it."

"Don't treat me like I'm made of crystal," Tabi tugged at a matted strand of Duncan's hair. "Or do you need to go look in a mirror and realize just how badly off you were when Jared dragged you in here?"

Duncan looked at her in surprise and then winced as he took in the state of his body.

"I'm a bit of a mess, aren't I?" He wrinkled his lip in distaste as he took in the gore and bloodstains that still marked his freshly healed skin. "And I thought you had a thing about blood?"

Jared burst out laughing behind her. "Wait, mouse doesn't like blood? Why didn't anyone tell me this? A vampire's lover doesn't like blood? Really? What, do you faint or something?"

"Yes." Tabi bit out the word with embarrassment. "Or get queasy. Sometimes both."

His laughter got louder and even Duncan began to chuckle.

"And that's why I don't tell anyone! I work in a hospital for fuck's sake. Do you think I'd ever hear the end of it if people knew?"

"I think you're in the wrong line of work, mouse."

"I do, too," Duncan kissed her again and then left the bed, moving carefully. "I think you should quit and then decide what you really want to do with your life. Take a month, hell, take a year or two and figure out what makes you happy. You're family now." He flashed a smile that showed his dimples and made her heart soar. "We'll discuss this further once Ruth's been dealt with, for now, I need to go shower."

Tabi looked around at the three of them and grimaced with distaste. "I think we could all use a shower. You two are covered in I don't want to know what, and I'm contaminated just by close contact."

"That is the best idea I've heard all night," Jared declared and the next thing Tabi knew she was being carried off to the bathroom.

"I didn't mean together! This house has more than a half dozen bathrooms for heaven's sake," Tabi argued but got no reaction other than male laughter and so she tried a different tactic. "We're not all going to fit in one shower. There's three of us, and I'm pretty sure Jared almost counts as two people all by himself."

"You clearly didn't peek around the corner when you used the facilities, or you'd know that wasn't true," Duncan commented from behind her.

She wasn't sure what he was talking about until Jared set her down and she realized that what she'd taken for an alcove for towels or something turned out to be another room entirely, one that was almost completely taken up by a massive, glass-enclosed shower. "You have got to be kidding me. Why does one man need that much room to shower?" she asked as she took in the black marble tiles and multiple shower heads. "This thing is sinful!"

"Not yet, but it will be in just a few minutes." Duncan winked and stepped past her to turn on the water. When he had the temperature where he wanted it, he stepped inside and then crooked a finger at Tabi as the hot water sluiced over his body. "Come on, lover. You're the one who wanted to get cleaned up."

Jared's arms snaked around her and he half walked, half lifted her into shower. Her back was to his chest and the hot water hit her from all sorts of interesting angles as Jared's lips found her ear and he nibbled his way along the curve and down to her lobe. "You're ours now, little mouse. That means we're both going to take care of you, in every way a man can."

"I'm going to have to quit my job just to have enough energy to keep up."

Duncan leaned in and kissed her, his mouth warm and wet. "If it doesn't make you happy, don't do it anymore. I'd say life is too short, but the truth is life is too long for people like us. You have lifetimes to look forward to."

"Lifetimes with the two of you." The idea made Tabi's head swim with the possibilities and her heart overflow with happiness. "I think I can handle that."

"Good. Glad to hear it." Jared nipped her earlobe lightly. "Now, shut up and kiss me too. We can talk later."

"Pushy!" Tabi yelped as his teeth closed on her ear again and then he was turning her around to kiss her, his mouth plundering hers as his big body sheltered her from most of the pounding water. Dizzy from the heat and blood loss, Tabi swayed a little and Duncan's arm curved around her waist and drew her up against him. "I have you, lover."

"Hold onto her will you? I have a plan," Jared grinned and began kissing his way down her body. His mouth suckled and nibbled at her breasts, feasting on them for a while before he moved lower, finally dropping to his knees so that he could kiss a ring around her navel before making his way down to her pussy. Her pulse was racing again and need was bubbling up inside her as she experienced the still new sensation of being with two men. Two sets of hands touching her, two beings devoted to her pleasure. The feeling was better than she could have imagined. The stubble on Jared's jaw rasped over her inner thighs as he nuzzled between them, his hands gently but firmly parting her legs until she was completely exposed.

"This is a sight to welcome a man home," he proclaimed before swiping his tongue over the length of her pussy, making her moan as sparks sizzled over her flesh at his touch.

He used his thumbs to part her labia and groaned with lust. "I may not be able to make you come just with a love bite, but I bet I can make you scream using just my mouth."

"No bet."

Jared's only answer was a wicked chuckle as he pressed his face between her thighs and began to devour her pussy. Duncan's arms stayed secure around her, holding her up as her knees gave way.

It only took a few flicks of Jared's talented tongue for Tabi to know that the effects of Duncan's bite hadn't completely left her system. Her libido roared back to life with a vengeance, soaking her cunt and setting fire to her blood yet again.

"Jared!" The wail broke from her lips before she could stop it and she felt more than heard his satisfied growl of response. The world spun and Tabi closed her eyes and fought against the urge to get carried off by the storm he'd ignited. As he drew the delicate pearl out of its protective hood and captured it between his teeth a bolt of raw lust shot through her and she screamed again, her entire body shuddering as she came. She'd never been a screamer before, but with these two, she couldn't seem to stop.

Starbursts were still dancing in her vision when Jared's hands landed on her hips, both men turning her around so that she was bent over with her hands braced against cool marble and her feet splayed far apart.

"Stay just like that." Jared's drawl was as thick as molasses, a sure sign he was not quite in control. She'd already learned that the stronger her men's accents got, the hornier they were. Tabi smiled to herself as she braced herself and then glanced over her shoulder at Jared. His chest had a mottled bruise rising over one pectoral. "You're hurt." She started to move and Jared shook his head, his big hands clamping around her waist. "It's already healing. Let me love you, Tabi. That's the only thing I need right now. I need to be inside you."

"Sexual healing is a song, it doesn't work like that in real life," she muttered as Jared draped himself over her to drop a path of butterfly kisses along her spine.

"It can work, when it's the right people," Duncan's hands stroked up the underside of her body to cup her breast as Jared's mouth continued to blaze a trail down her back. "When fate takes a hand, anything can happen."

Duncan found her nipples, tugging and rolling them

between his fingertips. Desire simmered and then flared and she leaned backward, pressing her ass against the steel shaft of Jared's cock.

"Don't tempt me," Jared warned her as he smoothed a hand over the curve of her bottom, working his finger into the crack to press against her anus for a brief moment. "Tonight's not the right time, but soon this pretty ass is going to belong to me."

"Duncan's right, you talk too much." Tabi deliberately wriggled against him and grinned when she caught the sound of his breath hissing over his teeth.

"You inspire me." Jared placed his hands between her thighs and spread her wide, rocking his hips so that the tip of his cock brushed over her slick entrance.

"Now who is teasing whom?" Tabi lowered her head and tried to rock backward but Jared's hands held her in place.

Jared finally eased himself into her body, moving so slowly that Tabi was trembling with need before he was halfway in. Duncan's hands kept up their tormenting touch, pinching and toying with her nipples until they felt hot and tingly.

"Please, stop teasing. Want you," she whimpered and flexed the muscles of her pelvic floor so they tightened around Jared's cock.

"Witch, stop that! I'm not going to stop teasing until you take back what you said about me talking too much."

Tabi's will weakened quickly. She turned her head to take back what she'd said, just so Jared would finally give her what she so badly needed, but then Duncan released her and she glanced up to see him give her a wink, a wicked smile on his leonine face.

"You do talk too much," Duncan announced and moved so quickly Tabi didn't see more than a blur. Jared's cock slammed into her as Duncan came around behind Jared and clamped a powerful hand down on the younger man's shoulder.

"But I know a way to shut you up." Duncan bit down on his own wrist and Tabi's lust skyrocketed as Duncan pressed his bleeding wrist to Jared's lips. Jared groaned as he lowered his head and drank. Tabi watched as Duncan's fangs dropped and his eyes blazed like tiny suns. For a second their gazes met and he smiled, baring his canines before sinking them into the heavy muscle at the top of Jared's shoulder. That's when Tabi remembered what happened when a vampire bit a human being.

Jared's moans were only partially muffled by Duncan's wrist and his gray-green eyes widened and blazed with the same inner fire as the vampire standing beside him. His cock grew impossibly bigger and Tabi felt her body stretch and give way as Jared began fucking her hard. Her head bowed and she could only brace herself against the forceful drive of his hips as Jared pumped into her again and again, completely lost to the sexual frenzy Tabi had so recently experienced herself. Jared's cock stroked her so deep he was hitting nerves she had never known she had, and every part of her pussy was throbbing in time to the wild, pounding rhythm of his thrusts. Strong hands gripped her hips, holding her in place as the room filled with the sound of flesh slapping flesh and the low howls of need being torn from Jared's throat.

Somewhere deep in the part of her brain that could still manage to think, Tabi knew that this was a moment that the three of them would remember forever. Something special was being forged here, linking the three of them in new ways. The thought filled her with joy and pushed her past every boundary of pleasure she had ever known and into heights so great that she felt as if her soul had been plucked from her body and bathed in a fountain of pure bliss. She added her cries to Jared's and her body clamped tight around his cock as she came in a shuddering rush that made the world go gray. Even then she sensed the moment Jared tipped over the precipice and joined her in ecstasy. She could feel his cock pulse with each jet of cum and she used her inner muscles to milk him for every drop.

Tabi's arms and legs were trembling and her body was still quaking with aftershocks as she slowly moved away from Jared and leaned up against the tiled back wall of the shower. She was tempted to collapse into a boneless puddle of sexually sated goo on the floor, but she wasn't sure she wouldn't simply melt away if she did that. Her two lovers moved to her side and gently held her up, each of them taking a turn with the soap and a wash cloth. They soaped and cleaned every inch of her with a gentleness that she could hardly believe. When they were done Jared held her close as Duncan cleaned away the last of the evidence of his injuries, and then he drew Tabi into his arms and kissed her as Jared cleaned himself up in turn.

She was more than half asleep by the time Duncan picked her up and carried her into the bedroom, toweling her off before tenderly putting her back in his bed. Jared had made it up with fresh bedding while Duncan had taken care of her. Once she was settled they both crawled under the covers, one on either side of her, and once again she found herself snuggled between two hard-bodied men.

"How are you feeling?" Jared asked.

She rolled onto her back and smiled as she found two pairs of eyes watching her every move. "I'm fine, really." Tabi scanned Jared's naked body and was relieved to see the bruise on his chest had nearly faded away. She gently traced her fingers over the spot it had been and then glanced over at Duncan. "So you healed because you fed from me, and Jared healed because he drank from you, but why did you feed from him when you wouldn't do it before when you needed fresh blood to heal?"

Duncan grinned. "I didn't feed from him, well, no more than a mouthful. He needed to heal too, and that wasn't going to happen if I took too much. As for why I bit him? He was taking advantage of your condition, so I thought I'd give him a bit of his own medicine."

"Bastard," Jared snarked and then laughed. "Though I suppose if Tabi isn't complaining, I really shouldn't be either. It was even better than I remember."

"Last time you were human, this time you're something more than human, so the effect is less...devastating," Duncan smirked at Jared. "You're welcome."

"Well it may have been less devastating, but I'm still wrecked." Jared kissed Tabi's cheek and got out of bed. "Keep the boss man company, will you? I need to lock down the house. There wasn't time to do it on our way in."

Tabi managed to haul herself to the top of the bed and wriggle back under the covers. She was already feeling the combined effects of interrupted sleep, blood loss, and the night's sexual escapades. She blew Jared a kiss and gave him a sleepy smile as he turned to head back upstairs. "Be careful."

Standing there without a stitch on and his clothes bundled under his arm, Jared grinned and winked at her, his body a study in masculine beauty. "Always am, mouse. Take care of him, dawn's coming fast. I'll sack out for a few hours once it's daylight and I'll see you around lunchtime."

"M'kay," she replied.

"Night, boss."

"Jared. Thanks."

"Keeping you alive, or at least mostly alive, is why you keep me around. See you at sunset."

Tabi listened until she heard the electronic beeping that indicated that Jared had left and resealed the door behind him. They were secure.

"I'm too tired to talk right now, but later on you and Jared owe me details on what happened tonight," she told Duncan before closing her eyes.

"Agreed." Duncan drew her into his arms. "It has been a great many years since I have had the pleasure of falling asleep with a woman in my arms. I'm glad you're staying with me tonight."

"Me, too." Tabi wanted to say something more. After what had passed between the three of them tonight, there was no doubt in her mind that was what she was feeling for both Duncan and Jared was more than lust and companionship, but she wasn't ready to put it into words yet. Instead she nestled her head into the curve of Duncan's shoulder and let herself drift back into the warm safety of sleep. She'd tell them tonight, when they were all together again.

CHAPTER 11

JARED GRABBED fresh clothes from his room and pulled them on quickly. The sooner he made sure the house was secure, the sooner he could head to bed. Even with Duncan's potent blood pumping through his body and healing the worst of his injuries and fatigue, Jared knew he needed a few hours' sleep before he'd be back to full strength.

He made his way to the upstairs security panel and checked it for alerts. Nothing. Not that he was expecting anything at this time of day. Dawn was coming fast and after the fight they'd had, no one on either side should be ready for another round just yet. He checked the windows in every room and made his way downstairs to do the same again, sweeping through the house and confirming that every possible way in was locked and barred.

As he headed into the kitchen he saw the non-perishable groceries still sitting where he'd left them on the counter what seemed like a lifetime ago. He started putting away the various cans and containers and then stopped as he remembered what else had been interrupted thanks to Ruth's interference. He and Duncan had made plans, and the implements of those plans were still sitting in the back seat of the Porsche out in the garage.

Not that we needed them, Jared grinned to himself as he replayed some of the highlights of their time with Tabi. She was an amazing woman, and tonight had been something incredible. Her presence in the house and in their lives was changing everything, even more so than Jared had thought possible. In all their years together he and Duncan had never repeated the intimacies of feeding, not since that first time. She was drawing the three of them closer together, deepening their bonds and forging new ones. He had no doubt that she was the love of both their lives.

"How the hell did we get so lucky?" he muttered to himself and set out for the garage. The rest of the canned goods could wait. He'd just scoop the toys from the car, stash them in his room and crash for a few hours.

His head was full of indecent plans of how to introduce Tabi to the toys he and Duncan had bought for her and so he didn't notice the single red light pulsing on the garage security panel until he'd already keyed in the code and opened the door. They were on him in seconds, and Jared only had time for a frantic swipe of his hand over the electronic panel before he was dragged into the garage, engaged in the fight of his life.

Somehow he managed to twist away from his assailants and face the security camera overlooking the space. Ignoring the pounding his body was taking, he looked directly into the camera lens and bellowed, hoping that Duncan would get the message. Then he turned to fight, already knowing that this was a battle he couldn't win. Not when the odds were three to one. Still, if he couldn't win, he was damned well going to try for a draw.

By the time they finally took him down, Jared knew that at least one of them would never rise again. One less for Duncan to have to deal with when he comes for them, Jared thought grimly as the concrete floor rose up to meet him.

Sorry, mouse. I should have been more careful.

TABI WOKE up to the comforting feel of a man's body draped over hers again and smiled. She was starting to get used to waking up this way. A quick glance at the clock by the bed told her it was nearly eleven o'clock in the morning. She untangled her limbs from Duncan's with care so as not to disturb his sleep. It amazed her to look at his perfect body and overlay the memory of what he'd looked like when Jared had half carried him in only hours ago. To look at him now there was no way to tell he'd been cut and bleeding and barely able to stand on his own.

Another hot shower in the decadent bathroom took care of most of her aching muscles, but she still couldn't shake the lingering sense of fatigue that clung to her. Not that it should be a surprise considering she'd experienced two significant blood losses in the last few days. There were bound to be a few side effects, but being able to heal Duncan more than made up for a day or so of feeling tired. He and Jared were the ones hunting Ruth, and Tabi was just grateful there had been something she could do besides hide in the basement and wait for them to come home.

With one last look at Duncan, she slipped a sweater over her head and went up the stairs to punch the unlock code into the keypad. Before she even got to the landing though, she could see something was different. The entire number pad was lit up with red lights, and when she tried to key in the code they had given her the night before it had made a series of snarky electronic chirps and the door stayed sealed. Tabi tried the code again, but it was no use. Well shit, now what was she supposed to do? Her phone was upstairs recharging, so she couldn't call Jared to let him know there was a problem. Assuming he hadn't already figured out there was a glitch.

A cold sensation slithered into her stomach as another possibility occurred to her. Oh shit, what if it wasn't a glitch? What if something had gone wrong? She sprinted back downstairs and launched herself onto the bed.

"Duncan, wake up!" She shook him and got no reaction. Shit! She shook him again and then remembered something from a long ago first-aid class and rubbed her knuckles sharply across Duncan's breastbone. "Dammit Duncan, open your eyes! Something's wrong!"

This time she got a reaction. Duncan's hand grabbed hers and trapped it against his chest.

"What?" He croaked the word and his eyes opened slowly. "Tabi, slow down. What's wrong?"

"The door! The door won't open and the keypad is flashing red and the code won't work and I think something's wrong!" The words poured out of her mouth in a panic-fueled torrent.

"Fuck!" Duncan snarled and sat up, and Tabi knew from the set of his jaw that she'd been right to worry. "How long?"

"It's just after eleven in the morning. I had a shower and when I went upstairs to meet Jared for breakfast I couldn't get out."

Duncan said something under his breath and then vanished from the room. She heard him swearing from the top of the stairs and chased after him. "I thought you were weak during daylight hours? You moved so fast I didn't even see you. That didn't look very weak to me."

"It's halfway through the day, so I'm about half-strength." Duncan didn't bother to look back at her as he answered. His attention was on the security keypad that was still flashing red.

"What's wrong with the door?" she asked.

"Nothing. It's working exactly how it should be." Duncan turned then and Tabi took a step back as she saw the pain and worry etched into every line on Duncan's face. "Jared's put the entire house on emergency lockdown. These doors won't open until five minutes before sunset."

"What? Why?" Fear twisted up her spine and soured her stomach. "Is Jared all right?"

Duncan reached for her then, gathering her into his

arms and pressing a kiss to her forehead. "No, he's not. If he were, he'd have deactivated the locks after the danger had passed. Since he hasn't, we have to assume something happened."

"No!" This wasn't happening. Jared had shown her how secure the house was. It was a fortress! "No, he has to be okay. Couldn't it just be a malfunction or something? It was nearly dawn when he went upstairs and this house is like Fort fucking Knox! Can't you override the door? Tear it off its hinges or something?"

"If I could, I would." Duncan hugged her tighter. "Hush, lover. I know. This isn't easy for me either. Jared designed this system because he took his duties as my guardian very seriously. I tried to have overrides installed but he had them taken right back out again. I hate the idea that he's out there somewhere and I can't help him. But we can try to find out what happened." He lifted her into his arms and carried her back downstairs at the same insane speed that he'd travelled up them. He set her down near his desk and ran his fingers under the underside. He flexed his fingers and part of the desk rose up, revealing a built-in flat screen monitor. Duncan pulled a keyboard tray out and began typing as Tabi crowded in close, trying to see what he was doing.

"The security system is linked to this computer. We should be able to access all the video feeds from here. Just give me a minute."

The monitor was suddenly filled with videos taken from all over the house and grounds and Tabi groaned as she realized this was going to take some time.

Duncan's fingers flew over the keys and more

windows popped up until Tabi wasn't even sure what she was looking at anymore. Frustrated, she started to pace the room like a caged animal. The deep pile carpeting absorbed the sound of her footsteps, and as she made the circuit around the room she tried to force herself to relax. She'd never had claustrophobia before, but knowing that she was deep underground and sealed inside wasn't sitting well with her. The large suite seemed to be getting smaller by the minute and the ceiling felt as if it were pressing down on her head.

"You're going to wear a hole in the carpet doing that. You need to calm down, Tabi, this is going to take a while, and even then we're more than four hours away from being able to get out of here. You might as well get comfortable." He glanced over his shoulder at her. "And drink more water. You're still recovering from last night's feeding and I am afraid I don't have anything for you to eat down here."

"Great." Tabi grumped, not bothering to hide her feelings. "Jared's in trouble, we're locked up, and I can't even have coffee? I'm going to kill this bitch when I get my hands on her." She paused in her pacing and glowered at Duncan. "And what did I tell you about telling me to calm down?"

Despite everything, the worry and the fear, Duncan burst out laughing. "Jared's right. You're a hell cat underneath that polished and oh-so-polite veneer."

"Now? You want to discuss this *now*?" Tabi pointed to the monitor. "Find out what happened and then we'll discuss my personality quirks!"

Duncan turned his attention back to the monitor, but

not before commenting, "And you can forget about getting your hands on Ruth. You are staying here where it's safe."

"Like hell I am! Last night there were two of you and you still came out half-dead. There's no way I'm letting you go alone!"

"I killed one of them last night and—shit," Duncan broke off.

"What? What do you see?" Tabi half ran across the room so she could look at what was up on the monitor. "Oh no. That's not...that's not Jared is it?" She grabbed onto Duncan's shoulder for support as the room tipped and slid away from her. There was a body stretched out facedown on the floor of the garage, but the angles made it nearly impossible to see the face, or even the head.

"It's not Jared." Duncan breathed a sigh of relief. "He doesn't own anything but runners and cowboy boots. Those aren't his shoes."

"Well, at least we know he didn't go quietly." Tabi looked past the body on the floor to scan the rest of the area she could see. "And he doesn't seem to be in the garage."

"I'd say they took him." Duncan was already typing in another command and suddenly the video jumped back in time. The body on the floor vanished and the dimly lit space seemed empty, until she saw a shadow flicker and a fast-moving shape darted out from underneath an SUV only to vanish again.

"What was that?"

"I'm not sure." Duncan was watching the video with rapt intensity.

Tabi noted the time stamp and frowned as she worked through the puzzle. "That's not a vampire though. Not so close to dawn."

"What I fought last night was a vampire, at least one of them was." Duncan's brow creased as he struggled to remember the fight. "But I didn't sense him at first."

"So what were you fighting?"

"That's how they did it," Duncan ignored Tabi's question and leaned in closer to the screen as the shadow reappeared and manifested into the shape of a tall man with dark hair and sharp features that reminded Tabi of a weasel. "He must have hitched a ride under the SUV as we drove in, which means he wasn't with the others." Duncan's eyes narrowed. "He was watching the house, waiting for us to come back. His finger stabbed at the monitor. "He's human, because no vampire could have crossed the threshold without an invitation. I think we've just met Ruth's guardian."

"He stayed hidden under your vehicle for ages. What the hell was he doing?"

"Waiting," Duncan answered as they both watched the stranger open the door of the SUV and activate the garage door opener. The rumble of the door opening could be heard through the computer speakers, confirming what had just happened.

"You have got to be kidding me," Tabi muttered. "You guys have a million dollar security system and all it took to get around it was a garage door opener?"

"We'll correct that oversight once I get Jared back."

"You mean once we get Jared back." There was no way Tabi was being left behind now. Duncan couldn't claim the house was secure, not after what they'd just witnessed.

"You're not coming with…" Duncan trailed off as the rest of the attackers stepped into view. The muffled sound of growls and gibbering spilled out of the speakers.

Tabi's bile rose and she took a half step back from the monitor. "What in the name of heaven are they?"

"They're called revenants and heaven had no part in their creation. They are an abomination." Duncan's voice was thick with horror. "What has she done?"

"What are they? They don't…are they even alive?" Tabi watched the creatures on the monitor in disbelief. There was something deeply *wrong* about the way the new arrivals moved, an unnatural glide to their walk as if their joints were fluid instead of flesh and blood. Their faces were grotesque, pale skin drawn too tight over the skull, sunken cheeks and lips curved up in a permanent snarl that showed their fangs.

"They're soulless bodies, reanimated corpses that do Ruth's bidding. I should have realized what she'd done, but last night they wore masks to hide their faces and I was too busy fighting to notice the clues. I should have paid more attention, I should have realized what they were…what she'd done!"

Tabi slid her hand under his hair and began to stroke the back of Duncan's neck to calm him. "I take it those things are not standard vampire companions?"

"No. Never. I'm not even sure how to make one of those, only that it involves using the recently dead. To make a true vampire a human is drained *nearly* to the point of death and then fed the blood of their creator.

When it's done, the fledgling goes through a feral stage where they are ruled by their appetites. If they are not guided through that time, or if their mind was broken to begin with, then the feral behavior can become permanent."

"That's what happened to Ruth, isn't it? There was something broken about her, and she kept it hidden from you." Tabi felt Duncan tense beneath her fingers and he paused the video before he answered her.

"She was broken beyond repair. Twisted in ways I couldn't see." Regret colored Duncan's words and he scrubbed a hand over his face. "Perhaps I didn't want to see it. I was lonely, and she was beautiful and fierce and I wanted her, so I took her and made her my companion, then my lover, and finally a vampire like me. I made her into an immortal killer, and gods, how she loved the kill." He stopped and sighed. "I should stop speaking about her in the past tense, since it is now quite apparent that among my other shortcomings, I failed to do my duty and kill her."

"Stop that right now." Tabi found herself moving so she could face him, her back to the monitor and their thighs touching. "You've carried all that guilt around long enough. It's time to let it go. She played you. It happens all the time. You're supposed to get up, dust yourself off and keep going. From what I've been able to figure out, you never got over it. You've been hiding away for the past seventy years and keeping everyone at a distance. When was the last time you went to see your sire? Why did it take you until tonight to do a proper blood exchange with Jared? For that matter, why did you ignore me, ignore everything we could have been? Because you've been feeling guilty, that's why." She leaned down and met his gaze, completely unfazed by the golden glow shining in their depths. "Get over yourself, Duncan Masterson. Stop living in the past. You've got friends here, people who love you!"

"Do you love me, Tabitha?" His hands cupped her face and held her so that she couldn't turn away, couldn't try and deny the words that had been hovering on the edge of her mind since the moment she'd seen him hurt and needing her.

"Yes." She dropped her eyes as she said the words aloud for the first time. "I love you, Duncan." Stripped bare of all defenses, Tabi stood and waited for the ax to fall. He'd send her home now, or tell her he liked her, too, or worse yet, just laugh and say nothing at all.

"Look at me." His voice was soft and a glimmer of hope sparkled in her chest. She raised her eyes and found his glowing brighter than she'd ever seen. "I love you." His thumb brushed over her cheekbone, wiping away a stray tear. "And as incredibly hot as it was to have you give me hell, in the future you're to remember that I'm the boss here. Got that?"

Tabi laughed and threw her arms around him as she kissed him. "Fine, you can pretend to be in charge if it makes you feel better, but I get to outrank Jared." Both of them went still as the mention of their missing third drew them back to the horrors of the present.

"I'll get him back, Tabi. I promise."

"Against those things? You're going to need help."

"There isn't anyone else near enough to get here in time. If I wait for backup they're going to kill him."

"There's one person you can bring with you. Me."

"No!" Duncan snapped at her as his eyes shifted to a darker shade of gold. "I love you too much to let you take that risk."

"You're not serious? That's your reason for leaving me behind? What about me? I love you *and* Jared, damn it! That has to count for something too! You don't get to tell me you love me and then use it as justification for making me stay here."

"Tabi, it would be suicide for you. You're human. You wouldn't survive that kind of battle."

Tabi made up her mind in that second, instantly knowing it was the right thing to do. The only thing they could do. "Then make me like you."

"You don't know what you're asking."

"Like hell I don't!" She couldn't believe he was doing this to her. Not now. "You already told me you wanted this for me one day, so don't you dare back down now. No take-backs!"

"I'm not turning you! Not like this!" Duncan's hands moved to her shoulders and he shook her lightly. "You'll be feral, violent. Hell, you'll be more than a little insane. What if you can't control yourself? What if you break and I have to hunt you down, too?"

"I'm not Ruth! You of all people know what my life has been like. You know I'm stronger than that. I can do this, Duncan. You have to let me do this." She stared into his eyes, willing him to understand, needing him to believe in her. She could do this. She had to. She wasn't going to lose either of them.

Duncan's gaze slid past her and back to the monitor. "This conversation is moot unless we figure out where he is."

Tabi wasn't going to let this go, it was too important. She had to make him understand. "No it's not. This conversation means everything. This isn't just about Jared. This is about you, and about us. All of us! Don't you see? You're still letting your guilt over Ruth affect your thinking. I'm not like her. If I was going to break, I'd have shattered a long time ago. If this is going to work, if *we* are going to work, then it's got to start right now."

"But what if—"

She laid a finger across his mouth, stopping his words. "No what-ifs. No doubts. You asked me to trust you, and I did. Now you have to trust me. I can do this." She moved in so close that their breath mingled and warmed the air between them. "When that door opens, I'm going after Jared. Whether I do that as a human or a vampire is your decision. So what's it going to be, Duncan? Do you believe in me or not?"

CHAPTER 12

THIS WASN'T the way he had wanted this to happen. Duncan had wanted to be able to introduce Tabi to this life slowly so that she had time to understand the sacrifices she'd have to make and the irrevocable changes that came with being a vampire. He'd wanted to give her time, not this frantic, pell-mell journey toward immortality and danger. It didn't matter what he wanted anymore though, she was right. It would take both of them to rescue Jared, and even then he wasn't sure they'd be successful.

As he looked into her eyes he could see the fear there, the way she held her breath as if waiting for him to tell her she wasn't strong enough, wasn't good enough to be considered worthy of his attentions. A lifetime of pain haunted her eyes and it made his choice an easy one. She was more than worthy. She was the bravest woman he'd ever known and the soul mate he never believed he'd find.

"All right."

"Thank you." She moved her finger from his mouth and replaced it with her lips, kissing him with unreserved joy. As he kissed her back, savoring the sweet taste of her, he wondered how he could have ever been fooled by the mask she wore. Tabi wasn't a meek little mouse, she was a lioness.

He hauled her into his lap and draped her long legs over the arm of the chair to kiss her again. Tongues tangled and lips teased as he enjoyed this moment with the woman he loved. It would be the last moment of quiet love they would have before they turned their minds to the war to come. He could only hope that when they came out the other side, the three of them would be together.

It was Tabi who finally broke their kiss, her fingers brushing his cheek before pointing to the monitor. "We need to see what happened next."

He slid an arm around her waist and leaned forward to click on the play button. They both sat in silence as they watched the video tell the story of what had happened while they had slept. When the revenants had rushed the door, Tabi grabbed his hand and squeezed it, never once taking her eyes from the screen. The creatures were louder as they attacked and Tabi nearly jumped out of his arms in surprise as animalistic snarls and grunts filled the air. Jared came into view a few seconds later, his fists dealing out terrible damage as he fought the creatures off.

Rage filled Duncan as he watched Jared being torn and bloodied, every sickening growl and sound of flesh hitting flesh only adding to his fury. By the time Jared turned to the camera and called out, Duncan was almost too far gone in his anger to catch the significance. It was Tabi who dove for the mouse and managed to pause the recording.

"What did he say? Rewind it and tell me if he said what I think he did! Why would he say that? It makes no sense."

"I'm afraid I missed it," Duncan confessed. He was struggling to get his emotions back under control. There was no time for the anger or the guilt he was feeling, but it was damned hard to watch his closest friend being attacked within the walls of his own home and not feel enraged. He set the video back slightly and watched again as Jared struggled and fought his way to a point directly in front of the camera, turning around so he was facing it dead-on as he yelled a single word.

"Why is he yelling 'Kojak'?"

"He's not." Duncan paused the recording so that Jared's upturned face was staring straight at them. "He's reminding me we're both LoJacked in a sense, at least our phones are. That brilliant son of a bitch is telling us how to find him."

He leaned around Tabi and called up a new screen, logging into his cellular account with a few rapid keystrokes. A few more clicks and a map appeared, showing two circles, one red and one blue.

"Gotcha!" He pointed to the blue dot as triumph pushed his earlier anger aside. "That's where they are keeping him."

Tabi leaned in and Duncan was almost certain he'd heard her growl in anticipation. "Then that's where we're going the second that door unlocks." She unwound his arm from her waist and stood up to reveal the look of determination on her pretty face. "Do what you need to do to make me strong enough to fight for Jared."

"I think you're already strong enough, at least in spirit." He took her hand and stood before tugging her back into his arms. "I'm just going to give you the physical strength to match."

Her hazel eyes stared into his and Duncan wondered what they would look like when they burned with the supernatural gifts he was about to give her. That would be just one of the changes this transformation would bring, and he could only pray that the woman he loved would survive it.

"How?" Her voice was soft but the tone was one of unwavering focus and he felt a swell of pride. This was his woman, and her courage was breathtaking.

"I'm going to make love to you, drain you and then at the point of death, you'll drink from me. You must remember to drink, Tabi. No matter how tired you are, no matter how comfortable it would be for you to drift away you *must* drink or I'll lose you."

"I'll remember." She smiled up at him and he tried to memorize every curve of her face, the tone of her voice, everything that made her human, so sweet, soft, and so terribly fragile.

"When you wake up, you must listen to me." He caught her chin in his hand and tipped her head up so that she was meeting his gaze straight on. "You'll be hungrier than you can imagine and you'll have needs so powerful that denying them will cause you physical pain, but you have to listen to me and do what I say. You must stay in control."

"I will." She smiled broader and her eyes lit up with laughter. "You're a real mother hen, you know that? Stop telling me what to do and let's just do this." She buried her hands in his hair and tugged his mouth down to hers with a kiss that was almost savage. Her teeth closed on his lower lip, nipping him sharply, and the slight pain sent a surge of heat straight to his cock and broke down the last of his will. She was his, and now was the moment he could claim her forever.

His mouth stayed mated to hers as he tore away the barriers between their bodies. Shredded fabric fell in tatters at his feet and he barely noticed. His fangs dropped into place and his dick sprang free as he ripped away his own clothes and pulled their bodies together in a heated tangle of lips and limbs. Somehow they made it to the bed, her legs wrapped around his waist and the wet folds of her pussy already rocking along the length of his cock as he followed her down onto the bed.

His hunger roared to surface, the twin needs of blood and sex kindling an inferno inside his mind and body and pushing every other thought aside. He craved her. He needed the taste of her on his tongue and the feel of her naked body beneath his. He wanted to hear her voice crying out in ecstasy as he sheathed himself in the hot depths of her cunt. Her hands were in his hair, holding his mouth to hers as she writhed beneath him. Every movement brought their bodies closer together, touching and teasing and stroking until his control shattered and he took her with one long, shuddering thrust.

"You are mine, now and forever." He threw back his head and howled his claim to the world before dropping his mouth to her neck. He could smell the blood pumping just beneath the surface of her skin and heard every beat of her heart as she turned her head and offered him her throat.

"Yours," she panted as the pulse in her neck leaped and jumped beneath his lips and then his teeth were piercing flesh and the hot blood was in his mouth. Tabi keened and arched up beneath him as the effects of his bite stole her mind and sent her hurtling into an abyss filled with exquisite pleasures. He'd experienced this moment a thousand, thousand times in his long life, but never before had it felt so right.

Duncan drank and drank as he fucked her, the world a dizzying whirl of erotic sensations as he sated his hunger. Tabi's cries spurred him on and he let her experience the full force of his desire, knowing that she needed him just as badly as he needed her. Their love-making was primal, fierce, and wild. Every thrust of his cock into her pussy sent him closer to orgasm, and finally his release came and he emptied himself into her womb as he took from her neck, a cycle of give and take that would bind them together forever. When his senses returned and his mind cleared, he felt Tabi lying still and quiet beneath him and he knew that it was time.

He rolled onto his back so that she was slumped against his chest and he held her there with one gentle hand as he tore open his own wrist with the other. He moved his hand to rest beneath her mouth and pressed the bleeding gash to her pale lips. "Tabi, you have to drink now. It's time, lover."

She barely stirred. Her only response to his voice was a faint moan and Duncan knew she was fading, drifting away from him toward death. He wasn't going to let go of her now, not when she was finally going to be his. "Tabitha! Drink, damn it. Don't you dare die on me!"

She stirred again and her lashes fluttered as her mouth sealed over his wrist and she drank.

"Good girl." He stroked her hair back from her face and blew out a shaky breath, barely feeling the pain of her feeding over the relief at knowing she'd passed the first milestone.

He let her feed until he was light-headed and then eased his wrist away from her greedy mouth, eliciting a soft, needy moan from Tabi.

"You need to rest now, my love," he whispered, and she must have heard him, for she went limp in his arms and sighed as she dropped into a deep and healing sleep. He knew she'd stay like this for at least an hour and likely more as the blood he'd given her altered her body and changed her forever. The mortal woman he had fallen in love with was gone, and in her place a predator had been born.

Once he was certain she was completely asleep he carefully rolled them both over again, withdrawing from her body and tucking her into his bed before he went in search of a meal, fresh clothes and weapons to use in the coming battle. As he headed for a set of little used rooms at the far end of the suite, he couldn't help but be grateful for Jared's need to plan ahead. Everything he needed was already near at hand, including a blood supply that would normally last a week. He had no doubt that when Tabi awoke, she'd devour every drop.

SOMETHING WAS TERRIBLY wrong with her. Even before she was fully awake Tabi could sense that much, but very little else. She tried to remember what had happened to make her feel this way, but it was like trying to have a conversation in the middle of a tornado. The words she needed were gone before she could grasp them and there was nothing but a terrible howling that pierced her to the marrow.

Hungry. Thirsty. Need. Want!

Carnal appetites surged through her waking mind and she sat upright with a wail. Need tore at her, burning her from the inside out and she couldn't think of anything else but the pain of wanting. Not even sure what it was she craved she started to crawl out of bed, only to feel strong arms wrap around her, holding her in place. No! She needed...needed something. She needed it to stop the pain, to stop the howling. She fought the one holding her, desperate to get free and then stopped as she recognized Duncan's voice in her ear, whispering to her in his softly accented words.

"Hush now, Tabi. Be still. I know it hurts, but I can make it better. Keep your eyes closed and do as I tell you. I'll take care of you."

The howling in her head was still there, a firestorm of needs and cravings she didn't understand, but Duncan's presence made it possible to think, at least a little bit. "Help me," she pleaded.

"I will. I am." She could hear the relief in his tone and wondered why he was relieved. She was sick, wasn't she? Shouldn't he be worried about her? His hold on her loosened and then something soft and slick was pressed to her lips. "Drink this. It will help."

She recognized the thing against her lips was a straw and drew it into her mouth. As the first sip hit her tongue she groaned as the most incredible flavor danced over her tongue. She drank deeply, greedy for every morsel and as she drank the fevered howling lessened just the slightest bit. Duncan held her, crooning soft words in her ear as she drained whatever he'd given her to drink. When it was gone she cried out in disappointment. "More! Need more!" The storm inside her began to rise and Tabi nearly sobbed in relief when a fresh straw appeared and she began to drink again.

The cycle repeated itself over and over until she'd lost count. Nothing existed except Duncan and the elixir that helped keep the howling emptiness at bay. When the pain had lessened and the screaming need within her had finally eased into something she could control, she finally remembered Jared.

"Jared. We have to save him!" She fought against Duncan's hold on her and was amazed when she was able to break away, scrabbling across the bed as she opened her eyes and stopped dead in her tracks. The world didn't look the same anymore. Panic welled up and she felt her control slipping as the tornado in her head began to spin again.

"Tabi!" Duncan's voice was steel and ice and she clung to it. "You must think. Don't react to anything you see or feel or sense. Do you understand me? Remember what I told you before you changed. You must remain in control."

Changed? Had she changed? Yes. That was why the world looked different, smelled different. She was something else now. The word flickered at the edge of her mind and she focused hard, fighting to remember what it was that she had become.

I am a vampire.

Fresh hunger bloomed as she remembered what she'd done, what she'd demanded Duncan do to her so she could help rescue Jared. Hunger. Blood. More! The bloodlust was nearly overwhelming but now that she knew what it was, it was easier to control.

"I'm still hungry," she murmured and for the first time heard the odd sibilance to her words. Her tongue swept over her teeth and she found her fangs, fully dropped and aching with the need to bite, to feed.

"I know, love. But you've already drunk more than you'd need in a week." Duncan moved around so she could see him, and she was dazzled by what she saw. An aura of lights flowed and flickered around him, bathing him in colors. "Your vision has changed, hasn't it?"

"Beautiful." She reached out a trembling hand to the glowing air that surrounded him.

Duncan took her hand and pressed a kiss to her palm. "I wish I could have prepared you better. Helped you to understand. You'll see more colors now as well as the infrared and ultraviolet, to a degree. You'll sense heat too, and your hearing and other senses will be amplified."

She nodded, already able to sense the changes.

"You're faster now, and far stronger." His touch sent ripples through her entire body, awakening another hunger just as fierce as her need for blood. Sex.

"Want you."

Duncan grinned, his own fangs flashing. "And I want you, but there's no time. You need to get dressed and armed, and then we are going hunting."

"Hunting." The word struck a primal chord deep in Tabi's soul. "Kill them, save Jared."

"Yes." Duncan nodded and the fire in his eyes gleamed as bright as liquid gold. "We're going to save Jared. But you must do as I say, and stay in control. You hear me? You must rule your appetites and not the other way around."

"I am in control." Tabi closed her eyes and visualized the howling storm of needs and lusts that raged within her mind and then mentally enclosed the whole thing in an unbreakable bubble of steel. Even then, she could feel it like an itch inside her head, so she added a wall of brick and mortar to seal it away and finally the roaring was muted enough she could think somewhat clearly.

"What did you do?" Duncan asked as she opened her eyes and grinned at him. "How did you...you're calm!"

"The power of visualization is a wondrous thing." She hopped off the bed and stretched, her mind relatively quiet for the time being. The rage and the hunger were still there, but they were simmering instead of boiling over. "So, you said something about getting armed?"

"I need you dressed first. I'm not sure I'll be able to stay focused if you're wandering around naked *and* armed."

Tabi laughed. "And you were worried I was the one who was going to be ruled by my appetites!"

Duncan just shook his head, a look of admiration and respect in his dark-honey eyes. "When this is over, you're going to explain to me exactly what you did."

"It's not going to hold forever, but I figure once we get the bad guys in view, that's not going to matter. I can unleash all this pent up energy on them."

This time there was nothing warm or gentle in Duncan's smile. "And so you shall. Just leave Ruth to me. She is my responsibility. And Tabi?" He got up and snaked an arm around her naked waist, tugging her hard up against his body. "Stay alive."

She kissed him, her tongue sliding carefully around two sets of fangs to tangle with his tongue. When he broke the kiss, she grinned, feeling more powerful than she'd ever felt in her life. "You stay alive, too. I just found you, I'm not losing you. Now, let's go rescue Jared from your ex."

CHAPTER 13

JARED COULD FEEL his life slipping away little by little and there was nothing he could do to stop it. Pain had been his constant companion since he had come to, and found himself a prisoner chained to a chair. He had welcomed the pain because as long as he could feel anything at all he could be certain he was still alive. Now even the pain was fading, and Jared could sense his death would come soon.

His heartbeat was erratic, and some logical part of his mind knew it was because there was no longer enough blood left in his body for it to pump properly. Ruth had wrung nearly every drop from him. It was impossible to know if he'd been captured hours or days ago, but he had to believe it had only been hours. He needed to believe that, because that meant there was still a chance Duncan would be coming for him. Duncan would come and destroy the abominations that filled this place and then heal Jared so they could all move forward with their lives, all three of them, together.

His mind drifted, barely tethered to his broken and bloodless body. Ruth hadn't been what he'd expected. The beautiful, brilliant and vicious vampire he'd once hunted across the world was now a twisted bit of decaying wreckage, mindless and unrecognizable. Her face and body were crisscrossed with scars and half-healed wounds, some of them still raw and oozing a fluid that reeked of decay. Her face was a death's head mask of taut skin and sunken eyes and her hair was a rancid tangle that cloaked her naked body. She had been brought over to feed on him, moving only when instructed to, and that was when Jared had finally understood. Ruth was a revenant, an animated corpse under the command of the vampire she'd created before her death. She hadn't escaped Duncan's justice after all.

The vampire had introduced himself as Derek and named himself Ruth's protégé. He was as unstable as his creator had been before Duncan had put her down, a creature of violent whimsy with black hair and dead eyes.

Derek had paced the ramshackle room they were all living in as if it were a palace, and his only care seemed to be for the welfare of the soulless shell of what had once been his creator. Derek treated her like a living doll, his own insanity making it impossible for him to see the truth of her existence. It had been almost a relief when she'd begun to feed, as it at least distracted Jared from the ravings of the madman as he wandered the room speaking of revenge plans decades in the making. Too drained and weak to even attempt to free himself, Jared waited and hoped again that Duncan would get there in time.

I'm not dead yet, but I will be soon. Better fucking hurry, boss, or it's going to be too late.

As if on cue a crash of splintering wood drew Jared's attention and he returned to the here and now. Too weak to even lift his head, Jared listened to the sounds of battle being waged all around him and thanked whatever gods were listening that Duncan had understood his last message.

Growls sounded, drawing his attention and Jared struggled to lift his head enough to see the fight unfolding just off to this left. The vampire's guardian was squaring off what had to be Duncan, but there was something off about Duncan's appearance. He was moving differently, as if the guardian was fighting someone else. Tabi? What the fuck was Tabi doing here and where the hell was Duncan?

Jared tried to make sense of what he was seeing, but his body was weakening by the second and it was a struggle to think clearly. That was definitely his girl standing toe to toe with the weasel-faced guardian, and she was holding her own, which shouldn't have been possible unless—

The explosive sound of gunfire filled the air and derailed Jared's line of thinking. He was almost certain that he had recognized the sound of his specially prepared shotgun being fired. Duncan was here too, and he was well armed.

A strange black fog was clouding his vision, but Jared was still able to make out the gruesome details as Tabi finished off her opponent by tearing out his throat. Blood dripped from her mouth, her fangs were bared and her eyes gleamed with a green light that could only mean one thing. His lover had become a vampire in the short time that he'd been gone. *Well, hell. I've only been gone a few hours and things have already gotten right out of hand.*

The shotgun thundered again, but this time the noise seemed muffled and distant. The dark fog cut off more of his sight and Jared summoned all his strength to call out to Tabi. He wanted to see her smile again, needed to tell her he loved her. He was dying. He could feel it. Not even Duncan's healing blood was going to fix things this time.

The world darkened to black and a terrible cold washed over him. Death was so close, but he wasn't ready to go yet. Not until he'd seen her. Not yet. Please, not yet. Something touched him in the darkness and then there was a sense of warmth against his mouth. A whisper of sound touched his ears and he knew it was Tabi calling to him from some faraway place. In the darkness a light bloomed and he followed it, chasing the sound of her voice. He still needed to tell her he loved her before he died.

THEY HAD MADE the drive in near silence. Duncan could actually see the jittering whirls of Tabi's emotions within her aura, and he was afraid that the slightest distraction might break the tenuous control she had over her appetites. She was nearly vibrating in her seat by the time he pulled over and they left the vehicle behind to make the last rush on foot.

It felt strange to watch her prowl with the grace of a predator, her fangs peeking out from beneath her upper lip each time she spoke. She was too agitated to be able to retract them, and her words were distorted as she tried to speak around their dagger-sharp points. He'd armed her with a pair of long knives and showed her how to hold them. There was no time for anything more than that. If they survived the night he and Jared would see to teaching her how to defend herself with a myriad of weaponry, or just her bare hands.

She prowled past him and he hauled her into his arms for one last, brutal kiss.

"You stay alive, lass. You hear me?"

"You fucking well stay alive too." She kissed him back, her fangs puncturing his lower lip just enough to draw blood and she groaned as she savored it. "I love you."

"And I love you. Though how in the hell I thought you were a quiet, shy thing, I will never know." He let her go and then they were running, flying over the ground so quickly no mortal eye could have seen them.

He spotted their target and turned, hurtling himself through the wood and glass door without slowing down. It shattered into splinters with a resounding crash and he finally stopped, seeking his target. Ruth.

Tabi flew past him with a scream of pure rage and went after the first target she saw, one of the revenants that had taken Jared. He forced himself to turn away from his lover and went looking for the one who had caused all this chaos and bloodshed. He reached out with his mind, but the once-familiar pattern of her thoughts was missing. It didn't make sense. She had to be here somewhere.

Something landed on his back with a gibbering howl and he could smell the rot of the revenant's flesh over the general stink of the place Ruth had claimed as her headquarters. He reached over his shoulder and flung the animated ruin of what was once a human being onto the ground in front of him, and his stomach twisted in horror as recognition dawned. Ruth was a revenant. He was still trying to process that fact as she staggered to her feet and came at him again, claws outstretched and her lips pulled back into a cadaverous snarl.

Duncan drew his sword and slashed, the move so instinctual that the blade was already carving through her neck before he truly knew what he'd done. Her head and body parted and tumbled to the garbage-strewn floor, and that was when he finally put it all together. If Ruth was nothing more than an animated corpse, mindless and broken, then there was another vampire somewhere in this hellish nest.

He could still sense his enemy's presence and he spun around, sword raised and his guard up, but it was already too late. The other vampire came at him from the side, charging wildly and using his body as a battering ram. The force of the impact sent Duncan staggering into a wall hard enough to cave in the half-rotted plaster, and his sword fell from his hand to get lost amid the refuse that covered the floor.

Duncan blinked to clear the dust from his eyes and got his first look at the vampire who had hurt Tabi and orchestrated Jared's capture. Lank hair, lean frame and the eyes of a madman stared back at him.

"You took her from me! You nearly killed her, my sweet love, my Ruth."

"I killed her, twice. What you did to her was far worse," Duncan retorted as he eased his fingers around the butt of Jared's shotgun.

"I saved her! She just needed to feed from the ones that hurt her and she would have come back to me! She told me herself, whispered it to me in my dreams." The other vampire howled with rage and hurled himself towards Duncan. "You took her away from me again!"

He didn't even have time to aim, just draw and fire and hope. The first blast took the wailing creature in the chest, knocking him backward. Duncan fired again, tearing away another chunk of the vampire's torso. Blood and flesh were scattered everywhere and for once the scent of it didn't make him hungry. He knocked the bleeding creature onto his back and stepped into the ruin of his chest, pinning him to the floor. Not bothering to try and find his sword, Duncan reached down and tore the vampire's head from his body bare-handed. Once the rage and madness in the creature's eyes finally faded, he hurled the gory bundle far from the torso. It was over.

As he turned to find his companions, a sorrowful whisper reached his ears and his victory turned to ashes and dust in a heartbeat as he sensed Jared's life force flicker and fade. He realized he was wrong. The battle wasn't over yet.

THE WAITING HAD NEARLY KILLED her. Every second they had been trapped in the basement had made it more difficult to stay in control. Her rage and bloodlust had howled and clawed at the mental walls she'd built, tearing them down almost as fast as she could rebuild them.

When the keypad had turned green they had been standing on the landing, both of them locked and poised for the moment they could start the hunt for Jared. Being free had helped for a while, as had the sense of finally being able to *do* something. While she'd been unconscious Duncan had pinpointed Jared's exact location, or at least the exact location of his phone. They could only hope he was still close to it.

The drive had been almost as bad as waiting for the door to open, and by the time they'd gotten close enough to go on foot Tabi had been literally twitching with the need to fight, fuck, or feed.

They'd left the vehicle parked close enough they could get to it quickly, but far enough away that their presence would not be sensed by the ones they were hunting. Tabi had never moved so quickly or effortlessly in her life and the three-block run had passed in what felt like seconds. She felt a strange tingle and instinctively knew she sensed the presence of another vampire. It was confirmation that they had found the nest and Jared. She was drunk with power and bloodlust, and the second they'd breached the door she had simply stopped fighting her new nature and let her instincts take over.

The plan had been simple. Leave the vampires to Duncan while she focused on the revenants and the guardian. Even in her half-wild state, Tabi had manged to keep to her instructions. She raced into the abandoned building with a battle cry, leaving Duncan behind as she launched herself at her targets and proceeded to tear apart the mindless creatures with terrifying ease, her strength and speed making it nearly impossible for them to touch her with fangs or claws. Logic screamed at her to be cautious, but the howling of her internal storm drowned out everything but the need to rend and tear and hurt the ones that had taken Jared.

Jared. She realized she hadn't seen him yet. She had to find him. Find him and make sure he was safe. She latched onto that single thought and held tight, trying to regain control long enough to locate him amidst the squalor all around her.

There! She spotted the red-gold of Jared's hair and started for him, but then the weasel-faced guardian she had seen on the video appeared in front of her, blocking her way. He stood between Tabi and Jared's slumped form, and Tabi's rage doubled, then doubled again and she tore into him with relish. She felt completely free, powerful beyond measure, and she gloried in it. As the guardian died she tasted his life on her tongue and part of her wanted to stay and savor it, to drink and drink until she was sated. The need to feed from her kill was almost overpowering and the world was painted in crimson light as she cast around her for another opponent to defeat, another life to take.

That was when she heard Jared calling to her. It was soft, so faint it was barely a whisper her mortal self would never have heard, but it was there.

The rage faded as she turned and ran to Jared's side. Even as she knelt beside him the storm within her ebbed and then quieted, and her thoughts were clear as she tore at the chains that bound him. He was alive, she could see that, but she could also see how little life was left in him. The aura around him was pale, his life force flickering like a guttered candle.

"Jared, you have to drink." She tore her wrist, ignoring the pain as she cut deeply and then pressed the wound to her lover's lips. "Don't you dare give up on me now. Drink! You're not going to leave me here with Duncan, are you? Who's going to take care of us if you go?"

She kept babbling as she eased him out of the chair and onto the floor. His big body was easy for her to lift now, and she hauled him into her lap and cradled his head in her arms as she held her wrist to his mouth. She threatened and cajoled by turns, pulling her wrist away when she saw him rousing. He moaned, and Tabi could have sworn her name was caught up in the low sound he made.

"Jared, I'm here. I'm right here."

"Hey, mouse," he croaked and his eyes opened a crack.

Tabi mustered a smile as she swiped at the tears tracking down her cheeks. "I leave you alone for a couple of hours and look at the trouble you get into!" she teased, but even as she spoke she saw the way his aura wavered and a sense of dread filled her.

"You two...okay?"

Tabi nodded. "I'm okay. Duncan will be here any second. Don't you go anywhere, you hear me?"

"Still pushy," he whispered. "Take care of him for me...promise."

Her heart twisted in her chest but she nodded. "I promise. But I'd rather you take care of us both." She let her gaze drift down his body and her worst fears were confirmed as she saw that his wounds had only partially healed. He was still dying despite the infusion. What was wrong? Was she too newly made? Was it only Duncan's blood that could save him? Where was Duncan! He had to stop this!

"Love you." The whispered words tore a hole in her soul and she bent over Jared and kissed his bloodstained lips.

"I love you, too."

Duncan finally appeared and dropped to his knees across from Tabi. "It's done," he announced and then sighed heavily as he saw the condition Jared was in. "You are a fucking mess, my friend."

Jared managed a faint smile but Tabi could see the light fading from his eyes. "Thanks for coming for me. Take...take care of her...for me." His eyes fell shut again and his next breath was painfully faint.

"Tabi." Duncan murmured her name so quietly only her vampire hearing allowed her to hear him at all. "He's too far gone for healing. We can't save him. But we can turn him."

Tabi answered in the same low tone. "He hasn't asked for that."

"And he's too far gone to get his consent now. Damn it, I don't want him to die!"

"Neither do I." She wouldn't let him die now, not when happiness was within reach.

"Then we turn him together and hope he forgives us for making the decision for him," Duncan murmured, reaching down to touch his friend's shoulder.

Tabi nodded in understanding and lifted her wrist to her mouth, reopening the still-healing wound as Duncan watched, his eyes grave.

"Sorry my love, but I'm not ready to let you go just yet," she whispered in Jared's ear and held her wrist to his pale lips. "Let us take care of you, Jared. You just drink."

For what felt like an eternity Jared didn't move and she wondered if he was too far gone to come back at all. Then his lips sealed against her wrist and he drew in a mouthful of blood. Pain burned through her as he began to feed, but it was nothing compared to the joy and hope that kindled in his heart as he began to regain his strength.

When she felt light-headed from blood loss Duncan moved her hand away and replaced it with his own, continuing the feeding until there was no doubt that Jared would recover. He would never be human again, but he was still with them. Or he would be if he forgave them for making him a vampire without permission, and if he survived his feral, fledgling stage. Hell, Tabi wasn't even sure she had survived hers yet.

They played catch up on the drive back. Duncan drove while she stayed in the back seat with Jared, his head cradled in her lap as she told Duncan about her fight with the revenants and then with the guardian. In turn he'd shared with her the discovery that it had been the second, fueled by an obsessive need for revenge, who had been behind everything. As insane and unstable as Ruth, he had brought her back as a revenant after Duncan had dispatched her so very long ago.

They'd made it back home without incident and settled Jared into Duncan's oversized bed after stripping the bloodstained and filthy clothes off him. Duncan had disposed of all their clothing and slipped off for a shower before taking Tabi's place at Jared's side so she could do the same. After that, they had eaten and then settled in to wait.

Jared stayed asleep far longer than Tabi had after her transformation, and every second they had to wait only added to her anxiety and tested her control. The battle had cleared her mind for a while, but now she felt ready to climb the walls. Tabi's whole world had changed because of Derek's thirst for revenge, but she knew it wouldn't be a complete life if Jared wasn't part of it.

She paced the length of the room, her mind whirling and her hands shaking with the effort to curb the need to rage and scream. She needed Jared to wake up and smile at her. To tell her he forgave her. She needed him to wake up before her control broke and she gave in to the howling storm of need inside of her.

Wake up, Jared. I need you.

CHAPTER 14

DUNCAN WASN'T sure which was going to make him crazy first, Jared's lack of movement or Tabi's frenetic pacing. He'd tried to reassure her that Jared's long rest was not surprising given the fact he was exhausted and badly injured before they had converted him, but it was plain that his lover was not going to calm down until Jared was awake. At least he hoped she'd calm down when he came to, because he wasn't sure he was ready to cope with two fully feral fledglings at the same time. As far as he knew, no one had ever been reckless enough to create two vampires on the same day.

Everyone kept telling me I needed to break out of my rut, he thought to himself. I'd say that's mission accomplished. He let his gaze wander from Tabi to Jared and back to his beautiful consort again, admiring the way her long legs peeked out from under the bathrobe she was wearing as she stalked around his quarters.

"Tabi, come here." He opened his arms to her and felt a sense of completeness as she bounded across the floor and into his lap, her arms twining around his neck as she buried her face in the crook of his shoulder. "You're making me dizzy with all the pacing. I know this is difficult, but wearing out my carpet isn't going to make him wake up any faster."

"I know, but I feel like I'm coming out of my skin and it's so hard to stay still."

"I promise this will get easier."

"Is he going to be just the same when he wakes up?" Tabi lifted her head, revealing eyes full of worry. "Why isn't he awake yet?"

"He'll be awake soon I suspect, and once he is he's going to be just the same as you were. Horny, hungry and ready to fight."

"Don't even say the word horny or I swear I'm going to jump you right here and now." She laughed and squirmed in his lap and Duncan's cock was instantly hard as she deliberately rubbed her soft ass over his groin. "What would Jared think if he came to and found us going at it right beside him?"

"Think? He's not going to be doing much thinking when he wakes up. Not everyone has your discipline, lover."

"I just kept reminding myself I needed to keep it together so we could get him back." Tabi leaned in close to Duncan's and kissed him. The moment their lips touched he felt the sharp tips of her fangs drop into place, betraying her fast-growing arousal.

"We got him back, and he's going to be fine. I just

hope he forgives us. I vowed I'd never turn another guardian. He knew that. I don't know what he's going to do when he comes around and realizes what we did. What I did."

"He'll say thanks for not letting me die," Jared drawled, his voice still rusty and thick with disuse.

"Jared!" Tabi was out of Duncan's arms and hovering over Jared in half a heartbeat. "You're awake! You're okay! Please tell me you're really okay."

"Not okay. Hungry. Thirsty."

"That's to be expected." Relief coursed through Duncan as he saw the light of intelligence in Jared's eyes. Not a revenant. He hadn't wanted to even give voice to the thought that Jared could have come back that way, but he had known it was a risk considering how close to death he'd been. He hadn't wanted Tabi to have to worry about it, not on top of everything else. Duncan snagged a blood pack from the stack he'd retrieved earlier and placed the tube to Jared's lips, grinning as he watched Jared devour it in seconds.

"More," was all Jared said for the next ten minutes as he proceeded to consume more than a week's worth of Duncan's stockpile. Duncan made a mental note to make arrangements for another delivery tomorrow. They were going to need it now that there were three vampires living in the house.

He was still contemplating all the changes that had been wrought in the past few days when Jared tossed an emptied blood pack off the bed and reached for Tabi with an amorous growl.

And we have now hit stage two.

Duncan shed his bathrobe and joined his two fledglings on the bed, pausing to make sure that the contents of the bags he'd found stashed in the back seat of the Porsche were easily accessible. He'd forgotten about Jared's little errand to the local sex shop yesterday, but now he'd found the goodies Jared had purchased Duncan had every intention of putting them to good use.

THE FRAGILE SENSE of calm Tabi had managed to sustain while taking care of Jared was shattered the moment he reached for her. Need surged through her like a dark and sultry poison that left no room for resistance. Not that Tabi intended to resist. She finally had everything she wanted and now she intended to celebrate by indulging herself to the limits of her new body.

Jared tumbled her to the mattress with a low, rasping growl as his hands tore at the tied-off belt of her bathrobe. When the simple knot defeated him he snapped the belt with a jerk and a snarl.

"In a hurry?" she teased, her skin tingling with the need to be touched.

"Can you blame him?" Duncan's accented voice rumbled from close by and Tabi turned her head to look for him. He was already stretched out beside them, his amber eyes glowing and his glorious body as hard and naked as Jared's. "I want you naked, too."

"Mine!" Jared snapped and Tabi jerked her head back to glare up at him.

"Get a grip, Jared! Don't you dare snarl at Duncan. I love both of you. Are we clear?"

Jared's gray-green eyes glowed brightly and he bared his fangs and snarled in frustration. "Trying...sorry."

"It'll get easier," Duncan's tone was reassuring instead of challenging and Tabi was grateful that at least one of them was completely in their right mind, because she sure as hell wasn't. Not by a long shot.

"Want you." Jared's words were slightly slurred as he tried to talk around his fangs.

"Want you, too. Both of you." She tangled her fingers into Jared's hair and pulled him down into a heated kiss as she half growled the next two words. "Right now." After that she couldn't have spoken if her life depended on it. Jared's lips sealed over hers, his tongue invaded her mouth, and his hands bracketed her shoulders as he ground the hard length of his cock against her pussy.

Tabi groaned into Jared's mouth and arched herself against him as the firestorm of cravings flared in her mind and broke through the walls she'd put up to contain it. She wanted her men inside her, claiming her, fucking her. The need was primal and raw and overwhelming, and Tabi gave into it completely. She clawed Jared's back hard enough to make him shudder and groan. She lifted her leg to wrap it around his waist, but then a hand caught her ankle and gently tugged her foot to one side, splaying her open beneath Jared's body.

"We have all night," Duncan reminded them both, his voice rich with amusement. "Might I suggest we don't rush?"

Jared lifted his head and grinned, his eyes still burning with green fire. "Are you going to start backseat driving my sex life now?" Jared asked of Duncan even as he started moving down the bed, pausing to kiss and nibble at Tabi's breasts as Duncan roared with laughter.

"God forbid. I think Tabi would kill us both if I tried."

"Someone is going to die very quickly if I don't get some attention here," Tabi complained and raked her nails down Jared's bicep for emphasis.

"Scratch me again and you're going to get a whole lot more attention than you bargained for," Jared warned. She didn't give him time to even lower his head back to her breast before she scratched him from shoulder to elbow.

Jared snarled and dropped his open mouth over one taut nipple, sucking it into his mouth hard enough she could feel the prick of his fangs against her flesh. He swirled his tongue around her areola and Tabi felt the contact all the way through her body to her clit, which started to throb and swell.

"Yes!" She arched her back and offered up more of herself to Jared's talented tongue. As her head pressed against the mattress Duncan's glowing eyes appeared about her and she smiled in invitation. "Hello, lover."

"Hello, my immortal consort." Duncan's words resonated in her soul and Tabi released one hand from its grip on Jared's shoulder so she could tangle her fingers in Duncan's blond hair. She drew him down for a kiss, their mouths open, tongues entwined, and even their mutual groans of bliss blended together. She drew Duncan's breath into her lungs and then cried out as Jared bit just hard enough to break the skin. The momentary pain added to her pleasure tenfold, and she was disappointed when Jared released her almost instantly.

"If he bites you right now, we'd have to peel you off the ceiling." Duncan chuckled and Jared joined in.

"Sorry."

Tabi groaned and squirmed in frustration. "Right. I forgot, too. Just...damn it, I need to come. One of you better step up to the plate or I'm not going to be responsible for what happens."

"All right." Duncan took control of the situation. "Jared, let her up. Tabi, hands and knees so your feet are off the edge of the bed. Jared, kneel in front of her. For your sake I hope she's better at resisting the urge to bite than you are."

"Bastard," Jared snarked as he rolled off Tabi and then helped her into position. "That's a nasty thing to say, even in jest!"

"Our Tabi wouldn't hurt us. She loves us." Duncan's voice was a sultry caress that rolled over her as she raised herself onto her hands and knees. "Don't you?"

"I do." Tabi lifted her head to smile at Jared and then glanced over her shoulder to where she could hear Duncan moving, but before she could catch more than a glimpse of her blond lover, Jared had her chin cupped in his hand and was kissing her softly. "I love you, too. You were the only reason I hung on as long as I did. I wanted to see you again. I just had no idea you'd be part of the cavalry coming to my rescue."

"She never hesitated, Jared. The moment we figured out what had happened, she demanded I change her so she could be there. We've got ourselves a hell of a consort."

"Yes, we do." Jared kissed her again, his kisses slow, lingering and so full of unspoken love that Tabi's heart was filled to overflowing. When he finally straightened up again Tabi found herself eye to eye with Jared's cock. Thick, hard, and with the tip already wet and gleaming with pre-cum. She carefully lapped at the head and Jared groaned, his fingers spearing into her hair.

She lapped at it again and then mewled in pleasure and surprise as Duncan's hands stroked up her inner thighs to tease the lips of her pussy.

"You're soaked already and we haven't even touched this pretty cunt yet," Duncan said and drew one finger along the seam of her swollen lips before sliding it into her folds to seek out her clitoris. He teased it out from its hiding place and worked his fingertip back and forth over it, sending delicious shockwaves through her entire body. Tabi moaned and sucked another inch of Jared's dick into her mouth, swirling her tongue over the mushroom-shaped head. She worked in more of him slowly, careful to keep her fangs from doing damage as she laved and licked at his cock.

"Yes, just like that. You have the sweetest, hottest mouth. Fuck that feels so good, don't stop." Jared's groans of encouragement and Duncan's finger on her clit were pushing Tabi higher up the pleasure scale. When Duncan's finger was suddenly withdrawn, she hummed in disappointment and Jared's cock twitched in response. Seconds later Duncan's fingers were back and something cool was pressed to her aching clit, and then she heard a click and her whole body arched in shock. Intense, incredible vibrations thrummed through her clitoris and up into her pussy and Tabi screamed as an orgasm tore through her with all the force of a hurricane.

With Tabi's control in tatters and her sex drive hovering around an eleven on a scale of ten, she lost all sense of herself and took as much of Jared's cock into her mouth as she could even as she pushed back against whatever Duncan had pressed to her clit. Her body shuddered as she deep-throated Jared, and when the faint tang of blood mixed with the taste of pre-cum and sex she barely noticed.

"Fuck!" Jared bellowed and she felt his cock thicken and swell just a few seconds before he came in a hot, salty explosion that filled her mouth with his essence.

"Oops." Duncan was laughing as he eased his hand out from between her thighs.

"Oops? She *bit* me and all you can say is oops?" Jared grumbled.

Tabi gave his cock one last stroke of her tongue before gently releasing him. "Blame Duncan. He's the one using...whatever the hell that was!" Tabi glanced back over her shoulder to see Duncan grinning at her.

"Don't blame me for using the toys Jared bought for you." Duncan lifted his hand, showing her the small device he wore over his index finger. "Nice choice by the way, Jared."

"Nice choice? Toys? What?" Tabi spluttered and spun around on the bed to glower up at Duncan.

"She's cute when she's irked." Jared drawled from behind her.

"She's gorgeous every second of the day, but she's exceptionally hot when she's annoyed," Duncan agreed and stepped up to the edge of the bed to gather her into his arms for a torrid kiss that melted her brain and made her forget what she'd been talking about. Strong hands kneaded her ass and pulled her up tight against the hard ridge of Duncan's cock. Tabi rubbed her cunt over his dick until he was slick with her juices and his breath was an unsteady pant that sawed in and out of his lungs.

The bed dipped behind her and then Jared's chest was pressed to her back, one hand sweeping the heavy fall of her hair to one side to bare her neck and shoulder. His lips touched her throat and she quivered, her pussy clenching, aching with the need to be filled. Hot, open-mouthed kisses left a trail of fire blazing across her skin and she moaned into Duncan's mouth. Duncan's hands shifted, parting her ass cheeks so that Jared could place a thick finger against the puckered skin of her anus.

"I'm going to take you there tonight, Tabi," Jared whispered, his breath fanning across her shoulder blade. "We're going to take you together and fill you so full you'll never want it any other way."

"Yes, please." Tabi wiggled her ass against the pressure of Jared's finger and felt a dark thrill as he pressed in past the ring of muscles. A fresh flood of honey flowed from her pussy and Duncan's nostrils flared.

"Can you smell her, Jared? Richer than perfume, that

scent. You've got her so turned on right now she's dripping wet." Duncan rocked his hips and his dick slid along the swollen lips of her labia, teasingly close to her clit but never touching it. "Do you want us to fuck you now, Tabi?"

"Yes." Her answer came out more of a whimper than a word, but Tabi didn't care. She just needed them to keep touching her, to come inside her, and make everything right between them.

"Tell us what you want us to do to you," Jared told her and slipped his finger deeper into her ass, wiggling it until she gasped.

"I want you to fuck me. I want Duncan's cock in my pussy and yours in my ass. I want both of you to love me at the same time and make me yours. I need us to be together, please. Make this forever."

Both men groaned in agreement and carefully withdrew from her body. Jared coaxed her back toward the middle of the bed while Duncan crawled past her to sprawl on his back, his cock jutting up from his body and every inch of him gloriously naked.

"How did I get so lucky? Not one, but two hotties all for me." Tabi brushed a kiss to Jared's lips and then laughed as Duncan patted his chest in invitation. "Poor man, are you feeling left out?"

"Left out, no. Horny? Fuck yes. Get up here and let us have you, lover. I don't want to wait any longer."

Tabi squealed as Jared took matters into his own hands and lifted her up and over Duncan, settling her so that she was straddling his hips and Duncan's cock was pressed firmly against her swollen clit. The contact sent sparks skittering into her womb and need bloomed hot and red inside her.

She moaned and swung her hips in a slow figure eight, grinding her pussy hard against every tantalizing inch of Duncan's shaft. Duncan groaned and reached for her, tangling his fingers into her hair and hauling her down across his chest. Golden eyes gleamed with the heat of the sun and he smiled, giving her a lust-inspiring view of both fangs and dimples just before he plundered her mouth with a kiss that drove the breath from her lungs and made her blood sing in her ears. Hot and demanding, his lips slanted across hers, his hand holding her so that he was in complete control, dominating the depth and intensity of the kiss. His tongue teased and tasted, thrusting in and out of her mouth like a preview of what he intended to do to her pussy. Unwilling to relinquish control, Tabi changed the angle of her hips and slid her body up and then back in a smooth, steady motion that had him buried to the hilt inside her cunt before he could stop her.

Duncan snarled and thrust up high and hard, lifting her almost completely off the bed. The movement pitched Tabi forward and she threw out her hands, bracing herself against the mattress.

"Perfect," Jared purred and Tabi felt something cool and slick being stroked over her anus. "Just stay still for a second, beautiful.

Tabi went still, her heart doing a slow somersault as she felt Jared's fingers ease into her anus again, first one, then a second. She felt a tingling burn as he loosened her in preparation, and then Duncan drew her head down for another kiss, nibbling at her lower lip and distracting her from what Jared was doing.

"So beautiful." Duncan's hold on her hair gentled and his kiss grew tender. "I will never feed from another. Everything I have ever wanted is in this room. I'm yours, lover."

"And I'm yours," Tabi whispered as tears blurred her vision and rolled down her cheeks. "Yours and Jared's. Always."

Jared's fingers pulled away and then his thighs were pressed to hers and his cock was right there, pressing against the puckered flesh of her ass. "Breathe out and push against me, mouse. This won't hurt. You're a vampire now, remember? You aren't going to feel anything but pleasure from this."

Tabi exhaled as Jared breached her opening and eased his thick cock inside. "Holy fuck, that's good. You feel so good, Tabi. So damned tight."

Beneath her Duncan groaned and his eyes glowed even brighter. "Tight and getting tighter by the second." His thumb brushed over her cheek, wiping away her tears. "No tears, lass. You belong to us now."

Warm hands encircled her waist and drew her gently backward as Jared seated himself deep in her body. "Ours," Jared vowed and bent over her as he worked in and then out of her ass, pressing her down into Duncan on each downward thrust. Soon the two men were working in concert and Tabi was pushed first one way and then the other as they fucked her together.

Tabi had never felt so full or as complete in her entire life. Home, she thought as her men moved together to bring all three of them to orgasm. This is what it means to really come home.

The slightest trace of pain seasoned the pleasure she experienced as Jared and Duncan's cocks stroked her in unison. Lust sizzled through her, nerve endings sparked, and every movement of either man sent another wave of pure ecstasy rippling outward from her pussy. Tabi flexed her inner muscles, clamping down on both men until they groaned aloud.

"Do that again, and you're going to get punished," Jared warned as his fangs grazed over the bare skin of her shoulder.

Goose bumps chased down her back and Tabi repeated the motion, milking both their cocks with a series of short, sharp pulsations. Jared snarled a broken version of her name as he bit into the curve of her shoulder just where it met her neck. Bare seconds later Duncan's fangs sank into her throat on the opposite side from Jared and both men drew in a single mouthful of blood as Tabi shuddered and then cried out as another orgasm washed over her and sent her spinning out of control. Caught up in the overwhelming pleasure of her release she didn't even realize she'd bitten Duncan until her mouth filled with blood. He arched beneath her, coming hard as her bite pushed him over the edge, and then Jared was joining them. They all soared together for one perfect moment, and then made the long, slow descent back to the world below.

"I'm dead," Jared muttered, his unshaven cheek tickling her back as he spoke. "That was too good to be real, therefore I'm dead and this is heaven."

Duncan chuckled and shook his head. "After the life you've led do you think there's any chance you're getting into heaven?" Tabi felt a tingling touch on her neck and she knew that Duncan was healing the bite he'd left in her throat.

"Valid point, boss. So if I'm not dead, then that means we can do this again."

"And again, and again," Tabi chimed in, blissfully content to stay sandwiched between her two lovers. "Just not for at least another hour or two. It's been a long day." She bit her tongue and healed the bite mark she had left in Duncan's neck with a few soft kisses, marveling at the fact that she had the power to heal.

"The house is secure. The sun will take care of the body upstairs and the fire will have long since destroyed the evidence of the nest. I think it's time we all rested." Duncan kissed Tabi's cheek and smiled at her, his eyes soft and his expression one of contentment. "Dawn is coming soon, and I for one am going to sleep better than I have in a very long time."

Jared eased himself up and off of Tabi and she watched as he padded over to the bathroom, admiring his naked ass until it disappeared from view.

She untangled herself from Duncan and flopped into a boneless heap beside him on the bed. Duncan laughed and got up to reorganize the bedding and fetched several homeless pillows off the floor and placed them back on the bed. Jared was back before he was done, and Tabi watched in sleepy-eyed amusement as the two men finished remaking the bed with her still in it. They each claimed a side and joined her beneath the covers,

Duncan's hand resting on her stomach and Jared interlinking her fingers with his before bringing her hand up to rest on his chest.

"So this is what it's going to be like from now on? The three of us together?" Tabi finally asked, needing to be certain that it was really as perfect as she hoped.

"Just like this," Duncan confirmed and Jared added a grunt of agreement.

"Then I just have two questions. First off, how much notice do you think the hospital needs when I tell them I quit, and secondly, if Jared's down here with us, who's going to be our guardian from now on?"

"Quit as soon as you're ready. It's not like you're going to need a reference." Duncan leaned up enough he could look at both her and Jared. "And as for a guardian, I think we'll be safe enough for a while. It's been brought to my attention that I haven't paid a visit to my sire in a very long time. I think it might be a good time for the three of us to go to London. Change of scenery, introduce you to my family... what do you say?"

Tabi squealed with joy. She'd always wanted to travel. "Yes, I say yes!"

Jared just groaned and threw an arm over his eyes. "I'm going to meet your vampire parents? Fucking hell man, if I had known that was a condition of this whole vampire gig, I may have opted for death."

Tabi elbowed Jared in the stomach and felt a moment of smug satisfaction as the air whooshed out of his lungs. "What he meant to say was yes, he'd love to come. Because he loves me and wherever I go, he goes."

Jared laughed and nodded in agreement. "Forever and ever, mouse."

"I'm bound to you for all eternity," Duncan vowed.

Tabi just held onto her men and smiled. She'd finally found her place in the world, and it was between these two men, forever.

ABOUT THE AUTHOR

Susan lives out on the Canadian west coast surrounded by open water, dear family, and good friends. She's jumped out of perfectly good airplanes on purpose and accidentally swum with sharks on the Great Barrier Reef.

If the world ends, she plans to survive as the spunky, comedic sidekick to the heroes of the new world, because she's too damned short and out of shape to make it on her own for long.

You can find out more about Susan and her books here:
www.susanhayes.ca